FUGITIVE'S VOW

Vendetta
Tangled Web
Inheritance
Trifles and Folly
Trifles and Folly 2

Night Vigil
Sons of Darkness
C.H.A.R.O.N (coming soon)

Other books by Gail Z. Martin and Larry N. Martin
Jake Desmet Adventures
Iron & Blood
Spark of Destiny (coming soon)
Storm & Fury

Joe Mack: Shadow Council Archives
Cauldron
Black Sun

Spells, Salt, & Steel: New Templars
Spells, Salt, & Steel, Season One
Night Moves
Monster Mash
Creature Feature

Wasteland Marshals
Wasteland Marshals
Witch of the Woods
Ghosts of the Past

FUGITIVE'S VOW

Assassins of Landria, Book 3

GAIL Z. MARTIN

Fugitive's Vow

Cover art by Adrijus Guscia. Additional art by Melissa Gilbert.
Print cover design by Melissa McArthur.

ISBN: 978-1-68068-234-2

This book is published on behalf of the author by the Ethan Ellenberg Literary
Agency.

This book was initially a Recorded Books production. Sound recording
copyright 2020 by Recorded Books.

Find out more about Gail Z. Martin's books:
Twitter: @GailZMartin
Goodreads: https://www.goodreads.com/GailZMartin
Newsletter: http://eepurl.com/dd5XLj
Blog: www.DisquietingVisions.com
Website: www.GailZMartin.com
Instagram: https://www.instagram.com/jmorganbriceauthor/
Pinterest: http://www.pinterest.com/gzmartin

DEDICATION

For my family, and my fandom family.

Acknowledgments

Thank you so much to my editor, Jean Rabe, to my husband and writing partner Larry N. Martin for all his behind-the-scenes hard work, and to my wonderful cover artists, Adrijus Guscia and Melissa Gilbert. Thanks also to the Shadow Alliance street team for their support and encouragement, and to my fantastic beta readers and the ever-growing legion of ARC readers who help spread the word, including Amy, Andrea, Anne, Carol, Dawn, Dino, Donald, Elizabeth, Jessy, Karolina, Laurie, Patti, Renae, Sandra, Sharon, and Trevor! And of course, to my "convention gang" of fellow authors for making road trips fun.

TABLE OF CONTENTS

CHAPTER ONE

"The heralds think they've been kidnapped," Ridge said, flicking the reins as he kept a watchful eye on the area surrounding the road ahead.

"They're not entirely wrong," his companion replied. "We were just polite about it." Rett tugged at the ill-fitting collar of his borrowed jacket, easing the way it rubbed.

"Henri will keep them fed and well-plied with good liquor," Ridge countered. "It's not like we just grabbed them off the street without warning." The horse and saddle, as well as his clothing, were not his own, and he felt acutely aware of every difference.

Rett rolled his eyes. "That's *exactly* what we did—and shoved them into a carriage before they could get their wits about them."

"It was for a good cause. And we did give them a warning," Ridge argued, shifting in the unfamiliar saddle to get comfortable.

"Telling someone 'don't scream or we'll all die—we're assassins, and we're here to help' isn't exactly what most people call a warning."

Ridge's lips quirked in exasperation. "What did you want me to do—tell them a bedtime story? We only had minutes to nab them. We had to grab first and explain later."

"I'm pretty sure they thought we were going to kill them," Rett persisted.

"Well then, think how happy they'll be when we don't." Ridge knew his smug smile pissed off his partner, which made the effort worthwhile.

Rett's look of annoyance was one of the constants of a chaotic universe, Ridge thought, feeling oddly happy considering their circumstances.

"Henri is probably going to offer to play cards with them after dinner."

"We'll make him give back anything they can't do without," Ridge assured him. "They should know better than to wager what they don't want to lose."

"You know Henri has that effect on people," Rett said. "He looks harmless."

"Harmless, my ass."

"No one figures that out until it's too late."

Joel "Ridge" Breckenridge and Garrett "Rett" Kennard had become legendary as King's Shadows, elite assassins loyal to King Kristoph. They had a well-earned reputation for breaking rules, defying convention, and blowing up far too many buildings. Their outstanding success rate won them lenience, much to the annoyance—and downright jealousy—of some of their fellow assassins.

In a business where most Shadows operated as loners, Ridge and Rett had always hunted their quarries together. Their friendship and absolute loyalty to one another were equally uncommon given their business. But Ridge and Rett had formed a bond back in the orphanage when they were eight and ten, and it had carried them through those days of hardship as well as their climb through the ranks in the army. Along the way, they'd made plenty of enemies, both among the traitors and criminals they hunted, and, by their unmatched record, within the ranks of their supposed allies.

Henri was their squire, valet, man-at-arms, and frequently co-conspirator. Clever, resourceful, and charming, Henri excelled at ferreting out information, acquiring resources by dubious means, and in a pinch, mixing poisons and driving a getaway carriage. Ridge doubted they knew the full truth of Henri's background, but what had been proven, time and again, was his courage and loyalty.

Now, Ridge and Rett wore the livery of Heralds of the Crown, posing as the official speakers for the king. The heralds proclaimed news and announcements in the town squares and city marketplaces throughout their assigned territory and passed along the information relay-style to their counterparts who bore that information on to the next area.

"You know the rest of the Shadows are probably wondering why we're not following up on the lead about the Witch Lord," Rett said.

Ridge snorted. "If they've noticed, they're probably glad we're absent. I'm happy we don't have to worry about watching our backs from them as well as from the traitors."

"You know they'd figure we finally got demoted if they knew where Burke sent us."

Ridge couldn't tell whether his partner sounded annoyed or amused. "Do you care? Burke thinks they've gone on a wild goose chase. You heard the case he laid out for us on this assignment. We've smacked the Witch Lord down twice now. He'd be smart to change tactics. And I've got to admit, attacking the heralds is brilliant in an awful sort of way."

"Yeah, well if Burke is right and someone is ambushing the heralds, there's no way anyone is going to miss us in these damned red outfits," Rett grumbled.

Since the heralds bore official news, they needed to attract attention. Their bright red jackets, black pants with a red stripe down the outside of the leg, and black riding horses guaranteed them to be noticed wherever they went. That was good for making proclamations and bad for avoiding brigands whose pattern of attacks seemed anything but random.

"Look at the bright side—since we're the professional assassins, whoever they hired to kill the heralds shouldn't be much of a threat," Ridge replied.

"Tell that to the six dead heralds."

Ridge was the older of the two and taller, with crow black hair and piercing blue eyes. Rett was two years younger and a few inches shorter, with chestnut hair and brown eyes. They had met in the orphanage when Ridge had taken Rett's side against a gang of tormentors, and together they had soundly whipped the bullies' asses.

Ridge taught Rett to read, and Rett taught Ridge to pick pockets. Except for the two years when Ridge had to go into the army ahead of Rett, they'd been inseparable.

The glint of the sun on metal alerted Ridge just in time. "Down!" he warned Rett as he heard the twang of a bowstring, and two arrows fired in quick succession. Ridge slid to the side, keeping a grip on his saddle even as he put the body of his mount between himself and the archer, then dropped to the ground and rolled into the high grass on the other side of the road, with Rett just seconds behind him.

Hand signals and long practice meant they worked in tandem silently, knowing each other's moves. Ridge went right; Rett went left and headed into the brush on the other side of the road, from where the archer had fired his shot. Their spooked horses galloped down the road, then slowed and stopped, waiting.

Whoever had fired on them had hiked in, because no parallel road was in view, and that meant he had either managed to vanish in minutes, or he'd gone to ground close by and hoped to outlast their patience.

Both assassins had drawn knives, easier to maneuver than swords with all the brush. Everything around them had gone quiet. Birds fled in the first flurry of movement, and no other travelers passed on the road. That left them and their quarry.

Ridge signaled to Rett, who nodded in agreement. Rett would play the waiting game, alert should their would-be killer break from cover. Ridge would stalk the bowman, moving sure and silent.

Ridge slipped through the brush, crouching to stay hidden. The land rose slightly, offering a hillock in a clearing full of low scrub and tall grass. It provided an excellent vantage point for the bowman but a difficult escape route. That the bowman had chosen it for his strike—and had still missed—reinforced Ridge's suspicion that they were not facing a trained professional.

Always make the shot, and always have a way out, he thought. *All the money they offer to pay is no good if you aren't alive to spend it.*

He surveyed the area, looking for where the archer might have hidden. The same lack of trees that offered good visibility provided no chance to climb into high branches or shelter under washed-out roots.

Where is he?

Ridge doubted the bowman was a complete idiot. Surely the killer had found a hiding place when he scouted out the site; even new recruits learned that.

Unless the Witch Lord's people are training their own, not drawing from the army's cast-offs.

Or the archer was good enough to be cocksure, and it never occurred to him that he might not kill his targets.

Ridge turned slowly, forcing himself to study the land. Where the small mound sloped down to meet flatter terrain, storm water had cut swales into the dirt, deep enough to give some cover and put a man below ground level where someone searching might miss him if he lay still.

A bird-call signal brought Ridge's head up fast, and he glanced across to see Rett peek above the brush long enough to signal toward a spot at the bottom of the mound. Rett was already moving in on the target as Ridge closed the distance, weighing the need to reach the same spot quickly against the necessity of stealth.

Ridge saw a shadow in the tall grass and glimpsed movement; then a figure came up behind and to the left of Rett, bow raised.

"Behind you!" Ridge shouted as he sent his knife flying, which crossed the gap faster than he could run.

Rett threw himself clear and rolled. He came up and sent his knife arcing through the air. His blade struck the attacker in the shoulder, even as Ridge's knife struck the man's thigh—aimed to wound but not kill.

They needed the attacker alive to interrogate.

By the time Ridge cleared the distance between them, Rett already had the stranger pinned, holding a blade to his throat. Although from the blood soaking the grass, Ridge didn't expect the archer to get back up.

"Who sent you?" Ridge growled. "Why did you shoot at us?"

Now that he got a good look at the bowman, Ridge felt even more certain that whoever among the Witch Lord's loyalists planned this attack had recruited civilians, probably farmers who used their bows to dispatch vermin from their fields or put a rabbit in the dinner pot.

The man stared up at them, clearly frightened and in pain. "A fellow came to my farm and offered me ten silver coins if I would shoot the two men in red. I needed money—I owed a debt. He said if I didn't, he'd see I went to debtor's prison and that my wife and son went to the workhouse."

"Who was he?" Ridge pressed, ignoring Rett's glance urging patience. Ridge could see from the man's pallor that he wasn't going to last much longer.

"I don't know. He was tall and thin, with a long face and dark hair. Not from around here. Don't know why he came to my farm, how he knew."

The man's voice faded as his breathing became more labored. "Knew it was wrong… didn't give me any choice." He stilled on the last word of his whispered confession.

"Shit," Ridge said, turning away. "Want to bet that even if he'd made the shots, there'd have been no silver coins?" Much as he hated the idea of someone hiring killers to murder heralds, Ridge also loathed that the masterminds pulled down-on-their-luck civilians into a dirty secret war against the king.

"Whoever hired him spent enough time in the area to find out who owed more than they could pay." Rett rose from where he'd knelt and bent over to close the dead man's eyes. "Someone might remember something."

Ridge shook his head. "Maybe—but we aren't going to get anything out of the locals dressed like this. Kane's the one who passed along the tip to Burke. Let's go home and see if they've found out anything more while we've been gone. We can always come back here when we blend in a little better."

Rett stared at the dead man, deep in thought. "I didn't pick up the touch of the Witch Lord on him. Did you?"

Ridge shook his head after he concentrated for a moment, opening his Sight, an innate ability to tell whether a person was soul-bound to a mage. Most often, when his Sight revealed someone to be mage-pledged, it was to Yefim Makary, the wandering mystic and self-styled Witch Lord—the man who posed the greatest threat to King Kristoph and the Kingdom of Landria.

"No. I don't either. I think he was exactly what he said he was— a desperate fool given a bad set of choices."

"Not like we can report that to Burke," Rett replied with a bitter note in his voice.

Ridge and Rett both had the Sight, a secret that could cost them everything—their rank as assassins, their freedom, even their lives. They had recognized the ability in each other as children and sworn themselves to silence. The Sight was a minor but powerful magic, something inborn that couldn't be renounced or removed. Rett's magic went further, offering him visions that provided glimpses of future or distant events. Their abilities had helped them save the king, the kingdom, and each other more times than they could count.

But magic was forbidden in Landria to everyone but the priests. Healers, mediums, and hedge witches existed on the fringe of the law, but they moved often and stayed mostly hidden, relying on their usefulness to keep from being turned in to the guards.

If Ridge and Rett were found out, Ridge feared they would be seized and forcibly recruited by either the priests or the army. Burke wouldn't be able to protect them, and King Kristoph might not care to take the risk on their behalf, no matter how much he was beholden to their bravery and skills. The Sight was just one more reason Ridge and Rett kept to themselves, making an exception for Henri and a few trusted allies.

They left the bowman where he fell and retrieved their knives. The horses waited in the shade a short distance ahead near the road, happy for a chance to graze.

"You think there might be another bowman out there, waiting for us?" Rett asked, although, at the moment, there was no one in sight.

"Doubt it," Ridge replied as he swung up to the saddle. "They're recruiting farmers, not deploying soldiers. If they cut deals with too many people, word would get around." He shook his head. "Even though the farmer didn't recognize the man who recruited him, whoever's behind this could be recruiting local informants, so they might already know who's vulnerable to push into a bad deal."

"What about the heralds? The people behind the bowman are going to figure out he failed. They'll try again. And we can't keep them locked up forever." Rett countered.

"Maybe they can change their schedule, take different routes, not go to towns in the same order as usual," Ridge replied, happy to shed the ill-fitting red jacket now that their ruse had accomplished its purpose. "Burke will know what they can alter without drawing the king's ire."

"The king isn't going to believe that someone is targeting his heralds," Rett said. "We've only just gotten him to believe in the Witch Lord. Kristoph is used to people who attack head-on. The Witch Lord manipulates, comes at things from a different direction. I don't think Kristoph's mind works like that."

"Then he's lucky he has us," Ridge said with a grin. "Because we're two sneaky sons of bitches."

Ridge and Rett took a table in the back room of the Ox Yoke Inn, where they had their backs to the wall and could see the doors. Since they were out of the hubbub of the main area, this location meant they could have a conversation without needing to shout. Both men had changed out of the highly visible heralds' uniforms into unremarkable outfits that would blend in among other travelers and stowed the borrowed clothes in their saddlebags.

All the better, since their business shouldn't be overheard.

"You think he'll come?" Rett asked, nursing his tankard of weak ale.

"He'll be here," Ridge assured him.

They had already finished a dinner of lamb stew, and while the main dish wasn't particularly memorable, the freshly baked bread and creamy butter hit the spot, and the wine was surprisingly not awful. The low hum of conversation filtered from beyond the doorway, punctuated now and again by a cheer from the latest winner at darts or raised voices in an argument. An utterly unremarkable evening, in an equally forgettable roadside tavern, outside a trading town where nothing interesting ever happened.

Which was exactly why Burke had arranged to meet them there.

Burke entered from the main room and sat at the table after he'd adjusted his chair for a better view of the doors. The Shadow Master remained trim and fight-ready despite being in his early forties. A scar through his eyebrow suggested he didn't shy from a brawl, and the gray at his temples and in his beard lent a distinguished touch to his appearance.

"Are the targets safe?" He dropped his voice to a low growl.

Ridge nodded. "Protected. Although how we'll keep them that way and let them go about their business, I don't know."

"I'll worry about that," Burke replied. "And the would-be killer?"

"Handled," Rett said. "Though it wasn't a fair fight."

Ridge heard the bitterness in his partner's voice and knew that it pained Rett when their orders and duty required them to kill someone neither one of them considered to be an equal opponent.

"The bowman wasn't a soldier or a trained fighter." Ridge stepped into the conversation to give Rett time to compose himself. "A farmer, most likely, pressed into the Witch Lord's service because he owed someone money."

A glimmer of something in Burke's eyes suggested that he understood why the death bothered his two best assassins.

"There's a cynical brilliance to that," Burke observed. "Harder to track, more difficult to anticipate who they'll pick next, and there's no oath to king and country we can draw on."

"The Witch Lord—he's dragging civilians into this," Rett said, and Ridge heard the heat beneath the apparent calm in the other man's voice. "Changing his tactics like this, he's got a new plan. We need to get ahead of him."

"Going after the heralds and messengers is shrewd," Burke admitted. "They carry the word of the king throughout the land. Most of them are legacies—in families that have served Kristoph's line for generations. Honorable positions, and essential for the kingdom to function."

Ridge nodded. "The people must trust that the heralds speak the truth and that what the messengers carry is valid. But killing the message bearers ... all news stops. The kingdom can't function."

"It goes beyond that," Burke said, speaking in a raspy whisper. "Just killing them wouldn't yield the outcome Makary wants. He must have someone in place who can influence the choice of the heralds' replacements. If he can put his people in those roles, they can alter the messages they bear and the tidings they proclaim. The experienced heralds and messengers would recognize that something was wrong and verify the information. The new ones won't. Makary will control what the kingdom knows and keep them from knowing what inconveniences him."

"Shit," Ridge muttered. Rett remained silent, but Ridge knew by the way the other man's jaw clenched and the hard set of his eyes that his partner understood the threat.

Ridge turned back to Burke. "We can't guard every herald and messenger—there wouldn't be enough of us to do the other work of the kingdom. Which no doubt, Makary knows," Burke growled. "We can't let him control the voice of the king."

"What do you plan to do about it?" Rett leaned forward, meeting Burke's gaze with an intensity Ridge knew too well.

"Not all news or messages are equal in importance," Burke replied. "Some pieces of information would be more useful for Makary to subvert. Our best bet is to provide extra security for those bearers."

"How?" Ridge shook his head. "There aren't enough of us, even if that's all we did—which the king isn't likely to support. Once people lose trust in the messengers, Makary wins the battle."

Burke raised his head, and Ridge could see in the other man's eyes that he knew the proposal was inadequate. "We'll just have to do the best we can while we try to run the Witch Lord to ground and stop his next attack. He's planning something, and meddling with the bearers is only part of it."

"I hate the way he keeps staying a step ahead of us," Rett muttered and drained the rest of his ale.

"He's been feeding misleading information where he knows our spies will relay it," Burke replied. "So the king sends soldiers and wants Shadows to help. When they get there, Makary is long gone. The information isn't coming from a single source, but when it's always wrong, it makes Kristoph less willing to take the next tip seriously—and cuts into morale."

"Which is why you've been sending us out on other missions," Ridge guessed.

Burke nodded. "You've been chasing the Witch Lord longer, and you're more familiar with how he works. If anyone is likely to find a pattern or notice a lead, it's the two of you."

"What now?" Rett asked.

Burke reached into his jacket and withdrew a folded piece of parchment, which he slid across the table. "Don't read it here. We have a lead on who Makary was before he became the Witch Lord, which may eventually explain why he is hellbent on destroying Kristoph—and provide some insight into a weakness. I need you to chase this down. There's no one else I trust to do it."

Ridge slipped the note into a secure pocket of his coat. "We'll get right on it."

"Don't come into Caralocia," Burke warned. "The city's not safe for you. You've thwarted the Witch Lord several times now. That makes you an obstacle keeping him from what he wants. Getting rid of you would make his plans run more smoothly."

"And we don't know who is on his side until they strike." Rett added the part Burke hadn't said out loud. Burke nodded.

Of course, Ridge and Rett had their Sight to fall back on as a warning, but that wasn't something they could tell Burke. The Sight also wasn't a perfect indicator; someone influenced at a lesser level than being soul-pledged would still be dangerous but not trigger a warning.

"How do you want us to report?" Rett had that wary, feral look that Ridge knew meant his partner felt uneasy.

"You still have a couple of the carrier pigeons?"

Ridge nodded. "Two."

"Good. Use those," Burke said. "In a fortnight, Kristoph will host a diplomatic event at Sommerelle, his northern palace. Be there, and find me. By then, we should both have information to share."

❀   ❀   ❀

Ridge and Rett waited a while after Burke left, watching the tavern patrons to make sure none of them followed him. They left more than enough coin for their meal and drinks and slipped out the back door, then rode for their most recent safe haven

The two assassins approached the house warily. Everything looked normal, but they had learned the hard way to verify. The unremarkable cabin had a small barn and a tidy vegetable garden. It would require a practiced eye to recognize that the "decorative" plants all had protective properties against magic and evil intent or to notice the small, detailed sigils carved into the wood at intervals to deflect hostile spells and unwelcome spirits.

"Henri?" Ridge called when they entered after they had seen to their borrowed horses and made sure their regular mounts received treats.

"We're in here."

They were welcomed into the cozy main room by a fire blazing in the fireplace and the scent of roasted chicken and onions. Lanterns on the mantle offered a warm light. An almost-empty bottle of whiskey and three glasses sat on the table. Three men held playing cards, but only Henri still had stacks of coins in front of him.

Two of the men were stripped to their boots and undergarments, having wagered and lost the clothing Ridge and Rett loaned them in exchange for their heralds' uniforms.

Henri remained fully dressed.

"Henri—" Rett began.

"Don't worry," one of the nearly naked heralds said, turning toward them and raising a hand as if to forestall judgment. "He said he'd give us back our clothes. He promised."

The bleary look in the man's eyes and the slur of his words made Ridge wonder if they'd started with a full bottle. Henri, of course, appeared none-the-worse for whatever had transpired. Then again, the two assassins had learned long ago that Henri could drink even much larger men under the table with no ill effects.

Henri was a short, balding man of indeterminate age whose pudgy build and round-plain face made him appear far more innocent and harmless than he was. His network of contacts among the shopkeepers, longshoremen, apothecaries, pickpockets, and petty thieves garnered valuable information and had saved their hides more than once.

He might not be an elite assassin, but Henri could be as quick with a knife as a cutpurse if the situation required and had proven himself to be an accomplished thief and lockpick as well. Ridge couldn't imagine their little household without their squire, who had truly become their third partner.

"Don't worry. I'll give them back their things," Henri replied with a smile. "It just made for a more lively game. Didn't it, boys?"

The two drunken heralds swayed in their seats with happy grins. Henri had managed to assure that their initially unwilling guests were unlikely to run off, and they didn't appear to be in a hurry to leave.

"I don't envy their headaches tomorrow, but it's much better than being dead," Ridge conceded with a sigh. "Nice work."

Henri gave the heralds back their borrowed clothing and led them to the large room in the back that held three cots, a wash-stand, and a chamber pot. It only seemed polite to let the heralds sleep off their drunkenness in relative comfort, since they'd been snatched to safety against their will. Ridge, Rett, and Henri could make do for the night in the front room, with one of them on watch at all times.

Once the heralds had passed out, the three of them gathered around the table. Ridge and Rett returned the heralds' uniforms, leaving them folded at the foot of their beds. Henri poured drinks and set out bowls of the roasted chicken and broth, along with chunks of fresh bread.

"Looks like you had everything under control," Ridge said through a mouthful of food.

"Not that we ever doubted," Rett added with a grin.

Henri shrugged. "I explained that they were in danger and then got them into a rousing game of cards. The time passed quickly—and the whiskey kept them from noticing," he said with a sly smile.

Ridge and Rett took turns recounting what had happened, including their meeting with Burke. "I did have a thought about protecting the heralds and messengers," Rett said when they had finished the recap. "There is a way that we could watch over them—and maybe help protect them as well."

Ridge gave Rett an assessing look. "Ghosts?"

Rett nodded. "There's no shortage of them, so having enough watchers to keep an eye on the message bearers wouldn't be a problem."

Ridge took a sip of his whiskey. "The heralds and messengers don't have your talent to see spirits."

"That doesn't stop the spirits from seeing *them*."

Ridge shrugged. "Good point. But why guess when we can ask Edvard. Or at least, you can."

Rett reached into a special pocket in his jacket and withdrew a worn coin. He held it in his hand and closed his fingers around it, shutting his eyes as he concentrated.

The air near their table grew cold despite the fire. Rett looked suddenly distracted, and Ridge gave him a questioning look.

"Edvard is here," Rett replied, dropping his voice. "I'll let you know what he has to say."

Edvard had been a trader who was suckered into smuggling and later murdered by those who had taken advantage of him. He had originally agreed to help Ridge and Rett bring his murderers to justice and stuck around because he enjoyed spying for them. Edvard had learned a few tricks along the way, including how to throw objects and momentarily incapacitate an enemy by walking through him. Those skills had helped to save Ridge's and Rett's lives more than once.

"He says that finding enough ghosts isn't the hard part," Rett relayed. "Lorella can even help the ghosts imprint on something easy to carry, like coins. But how do we intend to explain why we want the heralds and messengers to carry them? Magic is forbidden."

"Not a coin, perhaps," Henri mused aloud. "But a blessed medallion? The priests could hardly object."

"Burke might," Ridge pointed out. "And we can't explain it to him without risking our necks."

"Burke wouldn't have to know," Henri replied with a cunning smile. "I have an acquaintance who is quite the actor if the pay is worth the effort. He owes me a favor or two. Dress him up as a priest and send him to where the heralds and messengers wait to be dispatched. Have him give out the medallions 'for the protection of the gods.' If they've heard about the heralds who've been murdered, they might be eager for a little extra good luck."

Ridge grinned. "You're devious. I like that about you."

Henri made a joking bow. "I'm honored."

Rett tapped his fingers against the table as he thought. "It could work."

"We'd need to get enough medallions and take them to Harrowmont for Lorella to rally the ghosts," Ridge replied. "That's going to take a while, just to get there and back."

"Do you know how many you'd need?" Henri asked. "I might be able to get them from a friend."

Ridge raised an eyebrow. Henri's "friends" had a variety of dodgy talents. "Probably thirty. At least that would cover most of the messengers and heralds."

Henri nodded. "That's reasonable. I'll see what I can get tomorrow."

"We'll ride for Harrowmont as soon as we have the medallions—and we've sent our 'guests' back safely," Ridge added, with a nod toward the back room where the two heralds were passed out.

"Edvard also says to tell you that Kane's heading this way," Rett said. "We should remember to look surprised," he added with a smirk. Edvard's ghost vanished, and Rett replaced the haunted coin in its safe pocket.

Three sharp raps on the door alerted them to the arrival of their unexpected guest. Ridge went to answer it but glanced through the window, just to be sure. He stood aside as Kane slipped past him.

"I've got news," Kane announced.

He took the proffered glass of whiskey that Henri held out to him and knocked it back. "I have a lead on who Yefim Makary might have been before he styled himself as the Witch Lord."

Ridge nodded. "Burke told us as much—I thought it might have come from you."

Kane shrugged and flashed a cocky smile. "The less Burke knows about me, the better. Safer all the way around. But the point is, no one knows much about Makary before he started doing his whole mystic-from-the-wilderness performance. None of the abbeys claim him as one of the priesthood. We've suspected he's actually more educated than he pretends, but none of the nobility admit to knowing him."

"Does it matter?" Rett asked.

"It might."

"He wants to be king," Rett argued. "Seems pretty straightforward to me."

Kane raised an eyebrow. "Does it now? Why's that?"

Rett looked at the spy as if he were daft. "Because the king lives in a fancy palace with lots of money and plenty of food, and he gets to make all the rules."

"So if Kristoph got tired of being king and tried to hand you the crown and all that goes with it, you'd take it? Just like that?" Kane gave Rett an assessing look.

"Who, me? It might be fun for a little while, having the best of everything. But I imagine at some point, they'd want me to do king stuff, like go to council meetings and talk to diplomats. Don't think I'd be good at that," Rett said.

"Not to mention the whole people-always-trying-to-kill-you part," Ridge filled in, suspecting where Kane's mind had gone.

"Yeah, that too," Rett agreed.

"Exactly." Kane smiled like a well-fed cat. "Makary has been trying really, really hard to control the throne, but not be king himself. Too hard to just want luxury. So…does he want power? Wealth? What does he plan to do if he gets it? Strike down enemies? Make war with the other kingdoms? There's something that he wants besides just gaining the crown. If we understand what that is, we might have a better idea of how to stop him."

Ridge listened closely as Kane laid out his theory. He valued the spy's instincts, figuring that Kane survived by his wits in a rough-and-tumble underworld, so he had to be good at what he did. That Kane had something of a black sheep reputation didn't bother Ridge since he knew what kind of gossip circulated about himself and Rett.

"Suppose we find something. Then what?" Ridge valued information, but he didn't like the idea of leaving the hub of the action for too long on a research trip.

"That all depends on what you find," Kane answered. "I've got a hunch that he's tied somehow to the Bartleman family up in the Sholl area. The pieces I've put together so far suggest a connection, but it's not straightforward. That's where you come in."

"You're the spy; we're the assassins. You sneak, we shoot," Rett said, cocking an eyebrow.

"I've already been in that area poking around," Kane replied. "Gotten a bit too much notice, which isn't a good thing on a number of fronts. Time for fresh faces."

Ridge fetched a map and spread it out on the table, trying to remember where Sholl was in relation to their present location and Harrowmont, where they needed to go to take care of the medallion issue.

"Once we're at Harrowmont, we're not far from Sholl." Ridge pointed to the different locations. "We could make a circuit and still be back in time to meet Burke."

Kane's eyes slid to Ridge. "Let me guess. The event at Sommerelle?"

"Do you know something?" Ridge asked.

"I know lots of things," Kane smirked. "It'll be the first big event Kristoph will attend since the last attempt on his life. Rumor has it that he's a little nervous... can't blame him. That's why he's got the army and the rest of the Shadows looking under every rock for the Witch Lord. Except for you two."

"We don't play well with others. In case you haven't heard," Rett replied.

"There's a surprise," Kane muttered, but a faint smile touched his lips. Ridge didn't entirely trust him—then again, he didn't fully trust anyone except Rett and Henri—but for whatever reason, the spy seemed to have taken a liking to them. Maybe it was precisely because he and Rett didn't fit in with the rest of the assassins and military types.

"Is this all based on what you've dug up, or have you gotten anything useful lately from Malachi?" Rett asked. Malachi was a rogue mage, a necromancer who had helped on their previous mission. Ridge didn't know the nature of the relationship between Kane and Malachi, but he sensed a loyalty nearly as fierce as that between himself and Rett.

"There's a limit to what Malachi can do without putting himself at risk," Kane replied, and his expression shuttered at the mention of the mage as if that connection was one he carefully guarded.

"Unfortunately, it means he can't always do everything he might be able to do, if you catch my meaning."

Ridge and Rett had never admitted their talents to anyone except Henri and Lorella, their friend the medium. In spite of that, Ridge had no doubts that Malachi had figured out their abilities, and he strongly suspected Kane knew as well. That need for keeping magic a secret held even for someone as powerful as Malachi—perhaps even more so since energy of that strength might be too visible to the wrong people.

"Alright," Ridge said. "We can do this. How do we find you?"

"You don't. I'll find you," Kane said, with the smug confidence that annoyed the shit out of Ridge. The only thing that tempered his ire was that Kane really was that good at what he did.

Ridge looked over to Rett. "Well, glad that's settled. I guess you and I just go about our business and let everyone track us down."

"Works for me." Rett looked amused at the way Ridge and Kane inevitably ended up jockeying for dominance.

"I've got to go." Kane knocked back the rest of his drink and stood. "Be careful. Kristoph thinks he's closing in on the Witch Lord, but I don't think we can count Makary out yet. Don't let your guard down."

"We never do," Ridge assured him. Kane headed out, and they watched from the window as he rode toward the horizon.

"What do you make of all that?" he asked Rett and Henri.

"I think Kane knows more than he's saying," Rett observed drily, finishing his whiskey in one gulp.

"Of course he does," Henri replied. "That's a given. But I don't think what he's holding back affects you."

"I'd rather judge that for myself," Rett said.

"Maybe, but if you want Kane's help, it comes with conditions," Henri observed. "And I think what he adds appears to be worth what you have to put up with."

Ridge understood Rett's frustration, but he also appreciated Henri's cool-headed appraisal. "I don't doubt he's in touch with Malachi and that Malachi knows more about this whole business than they're letting on. The question is—does Malachi have a connection to the 'tower mage'? That might come in handy."

A mage of legendary power had been exiled for decades in a tower called Runed Keep. Details were scarce, but the best information Ridge had managed to pry loose said that the mage had failed to save Kristoph's wife and son after a difficult childbirth, and the king, in his overwhelming grief, had exiled the mage for his failure.

Whatever power the mage of Runed Keep possessed, Ridge felt sure it would be an asset in the effort to protect the king from the Witch Lord. Perhaps helping to save the king might atone for past failures and gain the mage his freedom. Ridge would have gladly made the case for allying with one another, but he had no sure way to get a message to the exiled mage.

"We might as well get some sleep," he said, seeing his fatigue mirrored on Rett's face. Henri seemed to have weathered guarding the "kidnapped" heralds with his usual aplomb, but Ridge knew the other man had to be tired as well. "We've got a long ride to Harrowmont tomorrow."

He glanced around the main room, taking in two benches near the fireplace and a worn settee. Henri gathered up the empty glasses and then returned to bank the fire.

"I'll flip you for the settee," Ridge said, eying the options. He figured the odds were high he'd end up on the floor by the end of the night, no matter the outcome of the coin toss.

"Take it," Rett said. "I'll sleep better on the bench." The loud snores of their drunken guests carried all the way from the bedroom. "Assuming any of us *get* any sleep."

CHAPTER TWO

"**W**e need a healer," Ridge growled when they reached the front gate of Harrowmont, Lady Sally Anne's fortress. "Fast."

The guards had been expecting them, courtesy of Edvard carrying a message to Lorella. Rett wondered if Edvard had also told Lorella to have a healer ready, that they were coming in wounded.

"Not much farther," Ridge coaxed, leading Rett's horse through the gates, while Rett concentrated on staying upright in his saddle. It wouldn't have been so difficult without all the blood loss.

Ridge twitched the reins, and Rett's horse stopped. In a flash, Ridge swung down from his saddle and moved to help Rett to the ground. Ridge had bandaged his wounds when they stopped outside of Sholl, the best they could do until they reached friendly territory.

"Of all the things that I thought might take me down, didn't think it would be a local cutpurse," Rett managed, trying not to sound like it was difficult to breathe.

"Nothing is taking you down," Ridge snapped. "And anyone can get in a lucky shot. You had him, and you made sure he didn't get back up. Just hang on, and we'll get you some decent care."

Ridge sounded angry, but Rett knew him well enough to understand that fear fueled the seeming fury. An assassin's life was dangerous, and they'd both been hurt plenty of times on the job, minor injuries as well as life-threatening ones. Ridge always passed off his injuries as nothing—no matter how severe, but he worried about Rett like he did when they were back in the orphanage. Henri usually tended to both of them after a fight, when they could make it back to wherever they were calling home at the moment.

Maybe that was why Rett heard an edge of what sounded like panic in Ridge's voice. This was the first time in a long while that they had to stay on the road after a serious injury. *He's just out of practice,* Rett told himself, even as his knees buckled, and Ridge took most of his weight to keep him upright.

"Stay with me," Ridge ordered, tightening his grip around Rett so that he didn't fall. "Not far now."

That's not fair. Long experience had trained both of them to act when the other one gave an order and argue later. That immediate response had saved both of their lives many times. Rett heard that tone in Ridge's voice, and everything in him tried his best to obey. He wanted to—but his body betrayed him.

He almost hadn't felt the knife wound when it happened, with the adrenaline high in the thick of the fight. They'd been ambushed not by soldiers or professional killers but by a band of thieves who had the advantage of eight to two. It wasn't until Rett had killed his attacker and tried to get up that pain flared through him, and he felt warm blood soak his clothing.

That shouldn't have happened. I'm one of the King's Shadows. He couldn't help feeling ashamed at having been bested by a simple thief.

Parts of what came next were hazy. Getting on his horse hurt bad enough that Rett fought to stay conscious. Moving with his horse's gait had been excruciating at first, but he'd grown numb as they rode. He'd seen the worried look on Ridge's face and remembered trying to smile, hoping to reassure. But after that...Rett lost track of time, recalling only snippets until they arrived at the Harrowmont gates.

Ridge hurried him up the steps and into the keep where Lady Sally Anne lived with those she had taken under her protection.

"We need help!" Ridge shouted. He eased Rett to the floor in the entranceway, then pulled back his coat and paled when he saw the bloody shirt. "We're going to fix this," he assured Rett, although

Rett could hear the tremor in Ridge's voice, and he knew from his partner's expression that the situation wasn't good.

Ridge pressed down on the bundle he'd made from his own shirt. He had told Rett to keep pressure on the wound while they rode. Rett remembered feeling the warm blood soaking through, saturating the linen, making him wonder how much was left inside him.

"Lady Sally Anne has healers. You're going to be all right." Ridge said the right things, but his panicked eyes told a different story. They had patched each other up too many times to remember, everything from minor injuries to far worse. Henri had an oddly comprehensive knowledge of battlefield medicine, as well as a network of dodgy apothecaries who seemed able to supply any potion or elixir needed to temper pain or cleanse infection.

Rett had done his share of binding wounds and keeping bedside vigils when Ridge was injured, white-knuckling it through the close calls. But Ridge had never lost the protective streak from when they were children, and their two-year age gap meant he shouldered the burden of responsibility for Rett's safety.

"Not your fault," Rett whispered. "I made a stupid mistake."

Ridge shook his head like he couldn't bear to hear that. "We'll fix this."

Rett heard footsteps coming toward them, several people, fast and determined. Ridge looked up, and all pretense left his expression.

"Help him," Ridge begged.

Rett faded out before he heard the answer.

Dark dreams followed. Rett recalled moments from their time in Sholl, gathering information to track the Witch Lord's former self. If people knew, no one wanted to say. That just made both assassins more certain that Kane's tip was valid.

The attack played over and over in his mind as if he could view it from different vantage points, standing outside himself. He watched himself react, saw the training kick in, as he and Ridge took on the brigands. They'd been winning. Then, it had all gone wrong.

For a while, Rett drifted. Each time consciousness returned, it brought different memories. The orphanage, where two boys from different families became brothers. The army, then their first days as Shadows. Too many near misses to count.

What surfaced next wasn't a memory or a thinly veiled nightmare. Visions felt different in the marrow of Rett's bones. If it was true that those on the cusp of death could see across realms without distortion, then Rett should have felt more frightened at the clarity of his vision.

He saw the sky fall, all blue with white clouds, crumbling around him, dropping away in pieces. Beyond the day sky, the night sky shone with stars until it too, crashed down and everything went black.

Oddly enough, the vision gave him hope enough to cling to.

It hasn't happened yet. I can't die here because I'm supposed to die there.

"Welcome back." Ridge's voice sounded odd, but the familiar sound helped Rett cast away the last of the cobwebs that shrouded his mind.

Rett opened his eyes, but he couldn't make out details in the darkened room. The only light came from outside the doorway, enough that it outlined Ridge but kept his face in shadows.

"Where?" He croaked.

"Harrowmont. You don't remember?" Exhaustion warred with worry in Ridge's tone.

"Not sure...was real."

"You've been out for three days," Ridge told him. "Even with everything the healer could do, it almost wasn't enough." The pain in Ridge's voice told Rett everything his partner didn't say.

"And?"

"She says you're going to be alright. It was a near thing, but you're a stubborn bastard." A hint of pride shone through beneath the worry.

"I made a stupid mistake."

"Forget it."

Rett knew it would take more than Ridge's absolution to forgive himself, but he'd take what was offered, for now. "I saw the sky fall."

"Meaning?"

"Don't know. A warning, I guess."

"One thing at a time. Get some sleep," Ridge urged.

"We've only got a fortnight." Rett had regained enough of his wits to know time was slipping away.

"We'll talk about it when you wake up again."

When Rett crawled back to consciousness the next time, he felt surprisingly normal. The pain in his side where the wound had been was gone, and the mind-fog of whatever painkiller he'd been given had cleared.

"Better?" Ridge tried for humor, but it fell flat. He looked haggard, unshaven, and with dark circles beneath his eyes, and Rett recognized all too well the signs of sitting vigil.

"Yeah. I think I feel alright."

Rett forced himself to sit up. He recognized the guest room at Harrowmont where he and Ridge had often stayed during visits. Two beds, a washstand, a table, and chairs. Nothing fancy, and everything necessary. A glance told him that the other bed hadn't been slept in, and the chair had been pulled near his bed.

They both looked up as a woman came to the doorway. "I see you're awake," she said to Rett and gave a nod of acknowledgment to Ridge. "I'm Renny, the senior healer."

Rett thought the healer might have been in her fourth decade. She was tall and spare, with high cheekbones and incisive blue eyes. Gray strands highlighted her short brown hair.

"You've been quite the project," she said, moving to Rett's bedside. Ridge drew back to give her space but did not leave. She sat on the edge and lifted the sheet to have a look at the bandage over his wound. Rett dared to take a peek. The area felt sensitive, but it didn't look nearly as bruised as he expected.

"I know you don't remember, but I did most of the work of knitting you back together that first day," Renny said. "After that, we had to fight off a fever and help make up for all the blood you lost." She felt for his pulse and placed a hand over his chest, monitoring his breathing. "Touchy business. Could have gone either way."

Renny gave him a look that made Rett wonder if the woman possessed other psychic gifts beyond healing. "How do you feel?"

"Like I got dragged by a horse," Rett replied, seeing no reason to hide the truth. "But better than when we arrived."

She nodded, and Rett wondered if she'd been testing him. "You're past the worst of it. Ridge already told me that you've got commitments elsewhere. I'd advise you to wait another day or two. It serves nothing for you to go out on the road too quickly and undo all my hard work." A twitch of her lips softened her words.

Rett cut his gaze over to Ridge, unsure how to answer.

"We're staying." Ridge's glare challenged Rett to argue. "You need to heal, and I need some sleep. Watching over you is exhausting." Ridge made a joke out of it, but Rett knew the reality had been bad.

Rett's worry over their mission must have shown in his eyes because Ridge just shook his head. "It can wait," Ridge said. "I need you at full strength when we head back out there. No telling what's waiting for us."

"Alright," Rett conceded, figuring it was an argument he couldn't win. "But while I recover, I want to hear all the news we've missed since we visited the last time. And we had some questions to ask if Ridge hasn't gotten all the answers while I was down."

Ridge shook his head. "Too busy trying to save your ass. Don't worry—we won't leave you out of the juicy gossip."

"Then my 'treatment' for today is for you to wash up," Renny said, wrinkling her nose a bit, maybe not just for emphasis. "And join us for dinner. Getting out of bed and walking a bit will help. You don't need to make a long night of it."

As simple as those two tasks were, they sounded huge to Rett, but he nodded. Even he could catch a whiff of sweat, blood, astringent, and healing herbs, an unpleasant sickroom smell.

"I'll have a basin of water sent up," Renny said as if she guessed his thoughts. "There's clean clothing in the trunk at the foot of your bed. Dinner is at seven bells. Lady Sally Anne will be expecting you—and looking forward to hearing your news." She glanced at Ridge. "Your partner hasn't exactly been chatty."

With that, Renny strode out of the room, and Rett felt like a sudden, powerful storm had just blown past them.

"She's pretty impressive," Ridge said, still looking at the doorway as if expecting the healer to reappear. "Very take-charge, even compared to Lady Sally Anne. After you passed out, she just swept in and took over—which was good, because I had run out of tricks."

Rett managed a tired smile. "You kept me alive long enough to get here. That counts."

"Yeah, well. I felt pretty damn useless," Ridge confessed. "I'm glad you were aware enough to send Edvard on ahead."

"I 'woke' him with the coin, and he figured it out from there," Rett replied. "If I'd had to explain things, we would have been out of luck."

Rett was steady enough to manage washing up on his own, a sop to his bruised pride since others had obviously cared for his needs while he had been unconscious. He felt better clean and figured that the lavender-scented water probably helped with the smell, as did clothing that didn't reek of sweat and blood.

He flinched as he raised his arms to pull a shirt over his head, reminding himself that the newly healed skin was still tender. Rett's fingers ran along the thin pink scar where the brigand had cut him. Thanks to the healer's magic, it looked like weeks, rather than days, had elapsed.

"I'm glad I could be of help."

Rett looked up at Edvard's words, but the ghost remained visible only in his mind. *Thank you.*

Edvard gave a shallow bow. *"My pleasure. It was good you thought to send me with the message. They needed time to prepare."*

I hadn't planned to dump a mess into their lap.

Edvard frowned. *"You and Ridge are in a dangerous business. Despite your skill and luck, sometimes things still go wrong. And even hurt, the two of you bested the robbers. Perhaps you were too busy fighting for your life to notice the ghosts of the other victims? Some could make themselves seen and felt, but most were too newly dead to be any help. None of them had gone far from where they died. Because of you and Ridge, those thieves won't be adding more to the graves beyond the tree line."*

Rett fought a shiver at Edvard's words. He hadn't been thinking about justice or retribution when the cutpurses jumped them; he'd just been trying to stay alive and make sure Ridge did the same. Normally, stopping highwaymen was the job of the king's guards, not the Shadows. He wondered if the thieves had any idea who or what he and Ridge were when they decided to rob them. He doubted it. That had proven to be a fatal surprise. Hearing Edvard's confirmation made him feel even better about killing the brigands, even if it had nearly cost him his life.

Ridge had given him privacy to get clean, but he returned in time to escort him to the dining room. While Rett had washed up, Ridge had done the same, even managing a shave, which Rett had not attempted. *After everything they've done to fix me, I'd hate to accidentally slit my throat while shaving.*

Neither of them mentioned that Ridge stayed a half-step closer than usual, in case Rett's knees buckled. Rett clenched his jaw, willing himself to make it down the stairs and to his seat at the large table, but he felt safe knowing that Ridge was within reach if he started to fall.

Lady Sally Anne, Lorella, and Renny were waiting for them and took their seats as soon as Ridge and Rett arrived.

"It's about time you decided to join us," Lady Sally Anne teased, although Rett felt her assessing gaze sweep over both of them. She and Ridge maintained a harmless flirtation, and Ridge usually primped a bit to look his best. That he'd barely managed to appear presentable gave Rett further insight into just how bad the past few days had been. Rett knew he looked like death warmed over.

"Always a pleasure to be among such gracious company." Ridge offered a lopsided grin.

"I'm just grateful to be up and about," Rett confessed. "Thanks to all of you."

As always, Lady Sally Anne wore a plain work dress likely made from the flax raised on her land. Her hair, blond with a trace of gray, wrapped around her head in a braid. Unlike the ladies at court, she wore no jewelry or cosmetics, but her attractiveness came from the character and determination in her features.

"Edvard was worried when he delivered your message," Lorella added. "He feared you would be coming over to his side sooner than necessary."

Lorella Solens's dark hair was caught up in a twist, and her eyes shone in the candlelight. She was a gifted medium whose abilities had helped them stop the Witch Lord's plans more than once. That made it necessary for her to seek sanctuary under the protection of Lady Sally Anne.

Rett shivered since Edvard's assessment had mirrored his own. "I'm glad it didn't work out that way," he replied.

Lady Sally Anne didn't hold with most of the customs of the aristocracy. Her kitchen staff brought food to the table, and those seated passed the platters and bowls, serving themselves. The meal she provided to her guests was the same as what was served in the larger main dining room, where all those under her protection ate in shifts. Those who found refuge at Harrowmont helped to maintain the fortress, working the gardens and laundry, learning bow and matchlock to defend the castle, tending the livestock and cleaning the barn, as well as serving in the kitchen and doing the housekeeping.

For most of the meal, Lady Sally Anne kept the conversation light, focused on the weather, humorous stories of day-to-day life within the fortress walls, and catching up on what news from the city Ridge and Rett had to share. Finally, after the plates had been cleared and they were relaxing with warm fruit tarts and glasses of good sherry, their hostess turned the talk to more important matters, and Renny excused herself to check on her other patients.

"What brought you this way?" Lady Sally Anne asked. "Much as we enjoy your company, you're far too busy to drop in without dire need."

Ridge nodded. "Guilty as charged, milady. We went to Sholl on our way here to investigate a lead about the Witch Lord. We believe he originally came from that area. If we could figure out who he was before he became Yefim Makary the mystic, our commander believes we might have better insight into what he really wants."

Lady Sally Anne regarded him with a look that made it clear she understood he wasn't revealing everything. "And did you find anything useful before you were attacked?"

"Unfortunately, no," Rett replied. "Although we were hoping that someone among your sources might know more."

"More likely someone among *my* sources," Lorella spoke up, meaning the ghosts. "Tell me later what exactly you are looking for, and we'll see what the spirits say. The dead have far less reason to guard their tongues than the living."

"Much obliged," Rett said. "The ghosts are the second reason we headed here. I'm hoping you can help." He laid out the danger to the heralds and messengers, as well as what they believed to be the Witch Lord's reasons for the attacks. "And that's why we were hoping to find spirits willing to attach themselves to the medallions we brought, to help us keep watch over the message bearers. They would be doing a great service to the king and kingdom."

Lorella leaned back and sipped her glass of port. "I'll ask. The attachment would need to be voluntary and temporary."

"Of course. We're not trying to take advantage of the ghosts," Rett clarified. "But soldiers can't be spared to accompany all of the message bearers for weeks or months, and the Shadows have been deployed to find out where the Witch Lord has gone to ground."

Lady Sally Anne looked at them thoughtfully. "Except for the two of you."

"We were just lucky enough to draw a special assignment," Ridge replied, with a hint of his usual charm.

"You'll be happy to know that the Witch Lord's trade in children with special abilities has waned—at least for the moment," Lady Sally Anne said, changing subjects. Rett had no doubt that she would eventually get the information she wanted out of them.

Ridge and Rett had rescued a number of children with budding talents as psychics, mediums, and telepaths who had been kidnapped by Witch Lord loyalists. Those loyalists wanted to enslave the children to enhance their fortunes or secretly convey messages. Sofen, a boy with particularly strong abilities, was one of the first children Ridge and Rett had saved. Sofen used his psychic talents to search for other such children who were being misused.

"That's good," Rett said. "Very good."

"Of course, it begs the question—why?" Ridge added. "Did the Witch Lord change tactics, or has Sofen been successful enough in getting the other children to safety that the supply dried up?"

Lady Sally Anne smiled. "For a while, a steady stream of 'special' orphans made their way here. Sofen trained some of the others to help him put out a 'call.' I don't know that we've found all of them, but the ones Sofen could identify, we've brought in." She shared a look with Lorella, and they both chuckled. "Let me tell you, it's made things interesting around here!"

Lady Sally Anne outlived an abusive husband and inherited his land and fortune upon his death, a demise that rumor held she might have had a hand in assisting. She turned Harrowmont into a sanctuary for other women seeking refuge, some of whom brought their children. Rett didn't doubt that the addition of Sofen and the other psychic orphans must have made for changes in what had been a fairly quiet daily routine.

Once dinner had a chance to settle, Lorella turned to Rett. "Are you well enough for me to attempt to contact the ghosts of Sholl?"

Rett wasn't feeling completely back to normal. Losing blood had taken a toll that would require rest and time to restore. But he did not want to wait. Their lives had a way of going in unexpected directions without warning, and Rett didn't want to lose the opportunity to seek the answers that prompted their journey.

"I'll be fine." Rett saw Ridge's worried glance and chose to ignore it. His stubbornness sometimes vexed both Ridge and Burke, but more often than not, it proved to be an asset when it came to the less pleasant parts of their job.

He doubted Lorella believed him, but until he passed out and fell over, they were going to have to take his word for it.

Lady Sally Anne and Lorella rose from the table and collected items from a sideboard, then arranged them in front of where the medium had been sitting. Rett recognized most of the ritual pieces from the times they had seen Lorella work her connection to the spirits.

Her studio in Caralocia had relied on props to impress paying customers, back before Lorella had been forced to flee when she ran afoul of one of the Witch Lord's wealthy followers. Now that she had no need for theatrics, the elements she required were far more simple: a silver chalice filled with water, candles, a mixture of dried herbs that helped to open a conduit to the other side, and a few crystals to strengthen her focus and protect her from malicious energies.

Lorella dressed as simply as her patron, in a homespun tunic and loose trews. But where Lady Sally Anne eschewed jewelry, Rett knew that the necklace, rings, and bracelets that Lorella wore were more than adornments. Silver, onyx, and agate had protective properties, while azurite, bloodstone, and turquoise helped to sharpen the focus of her abilities. She had taught him that much, trying to help Rett with his visions.

"How do you want to do this?" Ridge asked.

Rett knew that his partner believed in Lorella's talent, but seeing it at work, particularly when she opened herself to let the spirits inhabit her body and speak through her, still made Ridge deeply uncomfortable.

"I'm going to light the candles and burn the incense; then if we all take hands, it will help ground me," Lorella answered. "Edvard is with us, and some of the ghosts of Harrowmont. We are protected."

Rett wasn't a medium like Lorella, but as she lit the candles and spoke words of summoning to gather the spirits, he felt his power rise sympathetically. He hoped this wouldn't trigger another vision. The headache prompted by the last one had only just eased, and he still hadn't had a chance to figure out its meaning.

The temperature in the room fell, going from comfortably warm to cold enough that Rett could see his breath, despite the fire in the fireplace. Lorella reached out her hands, taking Rett's on one side and Ridge's on the other, with Lady Sally Anne doing the same across the table to complete the circle. Rett felt a frisson of energy that ran up his arm and down his spine. He wondered if Ridge and Lady Sally Anne felt the same but couldn't tell from their expressions.

A breeze in the closed room made the candles flicker and sent the flames in the fireplace dancing. Rett sensed new presences all around them, although he could not see any of the ghosts unless they made the effort to show themselves. Even so, the hair on his arms rose, and he felt an uncomfortable prickle on the back of his neck.

"We wish to know who the mystic Yefim Makary was before he took that name," Lorella said, addressing the host of spirits that came to her summons. "Surely one of you can say."

Rett had the feeling he was standing just out of hearing range of a group of people gathered in a nearby room. He couldn't hear individual voices or make out anything being said, but some part of his mind sensed a disquieting hum, as if the ghosts debated the question among themselves.

"Some of the ghosts hesitate to speak of him," Lorella translated. "Others argue over which answer is correct."

Abruptly, Lorella stiffened, and her grip on Rett's hand tightened. He had seen the medium channel a spirit before, but it always seemed creepy, as if it triggered a deep, primal wariness.

"I don't wish to claim that man as blood of my blood," she spoke, eyes wide and staring. Her shoulders squared, and her voice dropped in pitch, suggesting that a man's ghost addressed them.

"We pass no judgment on your family," Lady Sally Anne said with quiet authority, unperturbed. That led Rett to suspect their host had assisted with enough such events to be reasonably comfortable with the situation. "Tell us where he comes from so that we might understand why he seeks the crown."

They waited in silence, with Rett growing tenser as the seconds passed. He couldn't calm his uneasiness, and the vigilance that had kept him alive as a Shadow made him wary.

"His name was Thaddeus Bartleman," the spirit that spoke through Lorella said after a long pause. "Son of Arden, son of Toman. No one of any importance."

Rett knew that channeling spirits took a toll on Lorella; she would not be able to hold the connection long.

"Are there stories about why a man of no estate presents himself as a prophet to challenge the king?" Lady Sally Anne prompted.

"The Bartlemans never cared much for the kings of Landria. More than that, I do not know."

A cold gust tore through the room, extinguishing the candles and threatening to scatter the embers in the fireplace. Rett sensed a wrenching shift as if the tide had violently changed.

Lorella's grip tightened painfully, and her body arched and went rigid, head thrown back, eyes fixed on a terror only she could see.

"Lorella?" Ridge called out.

"Don't break the circle!" Lady Sally Anne warned.

Lorella gasped for air, twisting and jerking as if being strangled by an invisible foe.

"We've got to help her!" Rett protested.

"Let me try."

Rett heard Edvard in his mind, then caught a glimpse of the ghost rushing toward Lorella, colliding with the medium and then moving *through* her. For just a second, Rett thought he saw three figures all blurred together—Lorella, Edvard, and another man he didn't recognize.

The castle ghosts closed ranks, separating the stranger's spirit from Lorella, as Edvard slipped clear. Rett almost wondered whether the blood loss had caused him to see things, since none of the figures were solid, and no one else seemed to be reacting to the spectacle.

The intruder's ghost vanished. Lorella came back to herself with a gasp and slumped in her chair, letting go of their hands.

"Get her onto the couch in the sitting room," Lady Sally Anne ordered. Ridge waved off Rett's help and lifted the unconscious woman in his arms as if she weighed nothing. Rett followed him, standing back to give him room to maneuver Lorella onto the divan and arrange her comfortably. Lady Sally Anne sent someone to fetch Renny, then joined Ridge and Rett.

Ridge stepped away and looked in confusion from one of his companions to the other. "What just happened?"

"I think that after the ghost told us about Bartleman, another spirit showed up and tried to take over," Rett said. "I don't know what the intruder wanted, but Edvard came to the rescue."

"Edvard?" Lady Sally Anne raised an eyebrow.

Rett nodded. "He ran at Lorella at full speed and then went through her—and I think he pushed the other ghost out of her. It probably wore him out—he hasn't shown up again to report in."

"Not too shabby for a dead guy," Ridge said, respect clear in his voice.

Lorella groaned, and Renny appeared in the doorway. "Séance go badly?" Renny asked, hurrying over to check the medium for injury. Rett repeated his recap, and Renny listened closely.

"Possession by an unfriendly spirit is a hazard of being a medium. The question is—was it just a malicious ghost who saw an opportunity to seize a body, or did it want to silence Lorella because of what she might learn from the other spirits?" Renny asked.

Lorella opened her eyes and stilled for a moment, taking in her change of location. She drew a deep breath and relaxed into the cushions. "Well, that could have gone better."

"Could have gone worse too." Renny gave Lorella's shoulder a light squeeze. "How are you feeling?"

"Like a bone that two dogs fought over," Lorella replied.

"As far as I can tell, you're alright—physically. You'll have to tell me about anything else that I can't sense," Renny said.

Lorella was quiet for a moment, eyes closed as if assessing. "I'm more tired than usual. I fought against the other ghost, but I couldn't throw him clear. I'm very glad Edvard came to my rescue."

Rett hated to press for answers since Lorella looked exhausted, and he was nearing the end of his endurance. But he wanted to get the information before details slipped from her mind.

"Could you tell why the ghost attacked you? Did he want a body—or was he trying to keep you from learning something about the Witch Lord?"

Lorella turned to look at him. "It felt like he was afraid that the first ghost was going to say something else, because he didn't just try to take control of me—he ripped away the other spirit. It was…violent."

"What can we do to protect you?" Lady Sally Anne asked, worried.

"I don't think we have anything to worry about from that ghost," Lorella replied. "I believe the castle spirits will take care of that. It does make me wonder what was so important. The information didn't seem like much."

Ridge and Rett exchanged a glance. "We know someone who can take it from there," Ridge assured her. "Thank you. I'm sorry that it didn't go well."

Lorella pushed up to sit and shrugged at his apology. "This sort of thing goes with the gift. If it helps you find that maniac, it was worth it."

CHAPTER THREE

R idge insisted on staying two more days until he felt certain Rett had fully recovered, and Renny had given her approval. After Lorella's disastrous séance, the ghosts had been quiet. It had taken Edvard more than a day to regain enough energy to speak to Rett, although he was still too depleted to make himself seen. Rett was relieved that the ghost hadn't been harmed by the rescue, although perhaps it took something more drastic to hurt someone who was already dead.

"Here's hoping the ride back is a little less exciting," Ridge joked as they headed toward their latest safe house. "I wonder what Henri's been doing?"

"Probably set up three new hiding places, re-provisioned the existing ones, and did some digging among his contacts to see what he can come up with on the Witch Lord," Rett replied, enjoying feeling back to normal.

"I'm wondering what Kane will make of the ghosts' information," Ridge said. "There must have been more to what Lorella found out than it seems. We're missing something—I just don't know where to look."

"Maybe the ghost wasn't old enough," Rett mused. "Many of the families in the Sholl area have been there for generations. You know how people hold grudges. If the Bartleman family didn't like kings, perhaps there was an injustice done long ago, and Yefim Makary got obsessed with putting it right."

"Playing hero in his own mind?"

"Wouldn't be the first time."

Five days remained until the event at Sommerelle. Rett had a bag full of medallions, each with its own volunteer ghost observer. After Lorella had recovered from the attack, she had helped the ghosts connect to the medallions. The spirits weren't signing on to be protectors, she emphasized. Some might take that extra step, but it hadn't been a requirement. Edvard agreed to be the liaison, staying in touch with the observers and relaying news of any threats to Rett.

"I'm glad we got the charms for the heralds and messengers, but I hope we don't have to explain it to Burke," Ridge said as if he had guessed Rett's thoughts.

"If Henri's actor friend is convincing, then we won't have to. Let's just hope the message bearers are willing to carry the medals with them," Rett replied.

"You missed all the excitement," Henri told them once they tended their horses and headed into the safe house, hungry and exhausted from their ride. "Go, clean up, and I'll fix you something to eat. You'll want food and drink before I fill you in."

Curiosity came second to washing off the sweat and dust of the road and changing into clothing that didn't smell like a barn. Rett washed from a bucket on the back porch, leaving Ridge the basin in the bedroom. The cold water stripped away the fatigue of a long ride, giving him a second wind. Ridge looked equally refreshed when they reconvened at the table in the kitchen.

"What's this big news?" Ridge asked, settling down to a selection of cheese, bread, sliced meat, olives, pickled onion, and fresh butter. A pitcher of ale provided plenty to wash down the repast.

"The soldiers and the Shadows caught and killed the Witch Lord—or so it's been said." Henri sat back, arms crossed over his chest, smiling like a cat with a secret.

Ridge nearly choked. Rett spat a mouthful of ale and coughed to clear his throat. "Has Burke been here? Who's saying this?"

"No, Burke hasn't been here—which is why I'm not betting money that it's true," Henri replied. "And it's not the sort of news the heralds are going to shout in the town square, seeing how most folks never even heard of the Witch Lord. But that's the word from my...sources, what they've heard from the soldiers and the Shadows who were sent one way when Burke made sure to send you the other."

Rett didn't doubt Henri's "sources." He'd gotten solid information from them before. Rett figured they included the bartenders and barmaids, stable hands and squires, whose goodwill Henri carefully cultivated because they were the ones who went unnoticed by high-borns and criminals but who were in positions to overhear every careless conversation.

"What happened?" Ridge pressed.

"Someone got tipped off that the Witch Lord was meeting with his most devoted followers at an abandoned manor house out in the highlands. King Kristoph sent in the army, and if rumor is correct, the Shadows as well. Burned the place to the ground with everyone in it. No survivors and no one escaped."

Ridge and Rett managed an entire unspoken conversation with one raised eyebrow. They shook their heads in unison.

"I won't believe it until Burke can verify," Ridge said.

"I want to hear it from Kane," Rett answered at nearly the same instant.

Henri shrugged. "I didn't say I believed it. What matters is, does Kristoph?"

Ridge growled a curse. "Kristoph didn't want to believe the Witch Lord was a real threat to begin with. Then after the first assassination attempt, Kristoph didn't want to hear that Makary wasn't finished. But with this kind of 'proof,' Kristoph won't hear a word Burke has to say about a continued threat."

"Burke must have known there were plans," Rett mused. "And he very clearly sent us elsewhere. I'm betting he suspected it was going to be a set-up and wanted to keep us focused on the real thing."

"We'll find out soon enough at Sommerelle," Ridge said. "Assuming he doesn't come looking for us beforehand."

"Did you get ghosts matched up with those medallions?" Henri asked as he put away the leftovers. "My friend is ready to 'bless' the heralds and messengers as soon as you give him the goods."

"We got them," Rett replied, sparing the details. "The message bearers might need these more than ever if the Witch Lord just staged his death. People will lower their guard, and he'll be able to strike that much more successfully, which means the heralds are still in danger."

Henri took the bundle with the medallions gingerly, as if he expected the ghosts to pop out of the fabric bag. "How do you know they're really there?" He eyed the bag warily.

"I don't." Ridge shrugged.

"I can feel their energy," Rett said. "Lorella said she did it, and I believe her. I can pick up a sense of the ghosts' presence. And Edvard says it's real." Edvard hadn't tried to make himself seen outside Rett's mind since the incident at Harrowmont, and Rett figured the ghost was still recovering. He wondered how far Edvard's heroics had drained him and how long it would take before the ghost was back to full strength.

"Edvard's the key to making this whole medallion and ghost tracking scheme work, so I hope he's up to it."

Rett chuckled at the choice selection of rude words Edvard used to assure him he'd be ready. "He can hear you, even if you can't see him. Yes, he'll be up to it. Although his real answer was a bit more … colorful."

"Good. That's good." Ridge finished his tankard and tapped his fingers on the table. "Gods, I should be dead tired, but I can't stop twitching. I feel like we've missed something, like there's something waiting to happen."

Rett hadn't been able to shake that same feeling, although he'd chalked it up to the aftermath of everything that had occurred on their journey. "Maybe we'll be able to think a little more clearly after we get some rest."

⚜ ⚜ ⚜

Rett wasn't surprised when Kane showed up on their doorstep around midnight.

"Good. You're back," Kane said, pushing past Henri and into the sitting room. Henri had banked the fires, and they were just getting ready to turn in, following a few after-dinner games of cards and a couple more tankards of ale.

"This had better be worth barging in so late," Ridge grumbled. "We spent the last couple of days riding, and I'm a bit cranky."

That was an understatement, Rett thought. He'd fought beside Ridge long enough to recognize the mood. Hyper-vigilance, after the nearly fatal attack on the way to Harrowmont. Frustration that they hadn't learned more from the trip to Sholl for all its dangers. And something else that Rett had learned to respect—a twitchiness Rett knew came from intuition sensing a danger that was, as yet, undefined.

"Well, prepare to get crankier," Kane said, helping himself to a glass and bypassing the ale for the jug of whiskey they kept on the counter. "I don't think the Witch Lord is dead, and neither does Burke."

"Why isn't Burke here to tell us himself?" Ridge demanded.

"I wouldn't know. He doesn't tell me his schedule." Kane knocked back the whiskey. "But if I had to bet, Kristoph is running him from pillar to post trying to prove that Makary is dead along with his followers. Of course, since there weren't any eyewitnesses inside the mansion and mediums' testimony isn't legal, there's no way to know for sure."

"We ran down your tip about Sholl," Ridge said, leaning against the wall near the fireplace. "Even from the ghosts, there wasn't much."

Rett filled in what the ghost who spoke through Lorella told them. Kane nodded. "That's actually good. I needed a name. Somewhere in that family history there's a key to what we want to know—who Makary really is, and why he wants to unseat Kristoph."

"Well, you'll have to figure out how to interrogate the dead yourself, because we're fresh out of mediums," Ridge replied.

"I don't need ghosts. Local records will do just fine," Kane grinned. "The not-so-exciting part of being a spy. I'll head back up there and get to work."

Rett frowned. "I thought you needed us to go up there and poke around because you couldn't be seen?"

"And I won't be," Kane assured them. "I'll be a priest on official business. I knew I'd need to go back for this step—couldn't be spotted both times."

"Watch out for the highwaymen," Rett warned. "The king's guards don't seem to be doing much to keep the roads cleared. Although we helped out some."

Kane gave him a sidelong look, reading into what wasn't said. "I bet you did." He stood. "Thanks for the drink. Gotta go."

"You hear any rumblings about this diplomatic meeting at Sommerelle?" Rett asked, annoyed at Kane's brash entrance and quick exit.

"No, but I wouldn't expect to," Kane replied. "Boring business— a lot of deal-making and hand shaking. If you're asking whether any of the invited guests might be a danger to the king, not that I've heard, unless someone slips onto the list who shouldn't be there. I expect there will be high security because of who'll be attending, regardless of whether the Witch Lord is alive or dead. Now that I've got your lead, I'll be in Sholl—and I can guarantee the old archives will be more exciting than the discussions at that summit meeting."

Kane strode to the door, then turned, and his snide humor had vanished. "Watch your backs. Someone went to a lot of trouble to make it look like the Witch Lord is gone. You're going to be at the top of Makary's 'kill list' so that you don't get in his way again. If I hear anything solid, I'll make sure you know."

Ridge and Rett had already done their reconnaissance on the Sommerelle mansion days before the king's entourage arrived.

The old mansion had been in the royal family for several hundred years, and its earliest use as a defensive position could still be glimpsed in the remnants of the original wall and the watchtower that had long-since been converted to hold a large bell.

Over time, the need for a fortress had been replaced by the desire for a comfortable country manor to provide a change of pace from the main palace in Caralocia. Kristoph's predecessors had added on to the living area, making it spacious and comfortable. Sommerelle was not as rustic as a hunting lodge—of which Kristoph had two—or as formal as his other royal residences scattered among the kingdom's major cities.

The diplomats would draw up to the grand doors in their carriages, surrounded by servants, assistants, and the hangers-on that came with wealth and power. Royal guards would then escort the diplomats to the meeting area and would be stationed both inside the mansion and on the grounds. Ridge and Rett took note of all the access points and possible hiding places as they canvassed the location in advance of the event.

Although the manor house was ostensibly guarded at all times, with a minimal staff to keep the place tidy and provisioned between Kristoph's visits, Ridge and Rett had gained entrance with disturbing ease. The first floor held public rooms—a huge dining room, a grand parlor, several comfortable sitting rooms for private conversations, as well as a library and music room. The second floor had bedrooms for the visiting dignitaries, and the third floor held servants' quarters. The kitchen was in a separate building connected by a covered walkway.

"This doesn't look too difficult to guard," Rett said, slipping into the grand parlor with Ridge right behind him. Despite the mansion's beginnings as a fortress, effort had been made to make the expanded areas comfortable and opulent enough to befit a king. That included sprawling murals painted on the ceilings, large oil paintings hung on the walls, inlaid floors, and plenty of chandeliers to fill the rooms with light.

"It's not in the city, and there's nothing else nearby," Ridge replied. "That's a plus."

"If he uses the grand parlor for his main gathering, there's only one external wall," Rett pointed out, "and the servants' corridors only run inside one internal wall since the room isn't meant to host large meals." The hidden corridors allowed servants to deliver food and drink with minimal disruption, connecting to a main "secret" corridor that ran to doors near the kitchen.

"We'll have to make sure to have guards in the back hallways, regardless," Ridge assessed.

"I'm sure Burke will do that."

Ridge gave him a look. "That all depends on whether Kristoph puts Burke in charge. He's chafed at the restrictions to protect him from the Witch Lord. Didn't think it made him look strong enough. If he thinks Makary is dead, maybe he doesn't think he needs Burke as much anymore. He might not want reminders—which could include not being pleased to see both of us."

The thought had crossed Rett's mind, though he wanted to believe better of the king. Still, while Kristoph was, overall, a good ruler, impatience and vanity could get the best of anyone in his position. And despite the fact that most Shadows lived up to their title and remained unseen and unrecognized, Ridge and Rett had garnered Kristoph's personal notice after two dramatic and high-stakes rescues. They would undoubtedly be noted, at least by the king.

"Then we'll just have to prove we can be stealthy, for once," Rett replied. "Surprise Burke."

"Let's hope it's a nice, quiet evening. I would be thrilled for it to be completely boring," Ridge agreed.

After they had thoroughly canvassed the building—and eluded the servants, suggesting lax security—they returned to the safe house and found Henri jubilant.

"Amos delivered the best performance of his life," Henri chortled. "He out-priested the priests. No one questioned him. The clothing, the way he carried himself—it was a masterful performance."

"Your theater friend who was going to give out the ghost medallions?" Rett replied.

"A truly underrated talent," Henri gushed. "I've seen him on stage, and I believed he could play the role, but this … went beyond my wildest expectations."

An assassin's life left little time for niceties like the theater, and even if their schedule allowed it, neither Ridge nor Rett would have been comfortable in such tightly packed confines. Henri, on the other hand, often attended performances when Ridge and Rett were gone for periods of time. Rett suspected that Henri's theatergoing not only helped him pass the time but also enabled him to make and strengthen his valuable network of acquaintances from all walks of life.

"Did he pass out all of the medallions?" Ridge asked, intent on the results more than the manner of delivery.

"Yes. And he could have done with a few more, but scarcity made them extra valuable, and once he mentioned their protective properties, the poor man was nearly mobbed." Henri grinned broadly.

Ridge slapped Henri on the back. "Great job. Just what do we owe your friend?"

"A jug of decent whiskey will go a long way—actor, remember?" Henri replied. "He owed me several favors, so this worked off part of his debt."

"The real question is—if the Witch Lord isn't dead, did he narrowly escape a true attack, or was the whole thing a set-up to give Kristoph false confidence, and the real danger is still ahead?" Rett wondered aloud.

"If Burke and Kane are right, my money's on the latter." Ridge folded his arms and leaned against the wall. "And Sommerelle is the next big thing—Kristoph out of the palace and off his usual routine."

"Even before the Witch Lord, the king always had protection. So Kristoph isn't likely to show up without guards."

"He won't bring an army to a diplomatic event—and now that he thinks the big problem is solved, he doesn't think he needs to," Ridge countered. "So we're just going to have to be the army."

It's not just the two of you," Henri spoke up. "Edvard and I will be close enough to lend a hand."

"Thanks," Rett replied, smiling. Henri had proven he could be an asset under tough circumstances, and Edvard could move unseen to help with surveillance. They had pulled off wins before, against the odds. Rett just hoped their luck held.

At first, Rett worried that Kristoph would recognize him as one of the Shadows. Then he realized that the king scarcely noticed the servants who bustled at the sidelines to make his grand diplomatic meeting a success, and Rett was dressed as one of the servers. No one appeared to be on the lookout for ghosts either, since Edvard encountered no evidence of any supernatural warding during his circuit of the building.

Ridge positioned himself outside, where he had a vantage point of the kitchen and rear entrance, since the king's guards stood sentry at the front doors, checking all the guests as they entered. So far, Rett hadn't caught sight of Burke or any of the other Shadows. He wondered if Burke had intentionally not made contact so that he could deny having given the order for Ridge and Rett to attend, should Kristoph notice.

Not to leave us to face the king's wrath; more like a good excuse why he didn't tell us not to come, he thought.

Rett hadn't experienced a vision since the one at Harrowmont, but the memory bothered him. Despite confirming that nothing seemed amiss, Rett couldn't shake the warning of his intuition. His gut told him something bad was going to happen, even if he could find no evidence to support his fears.

Once more, he scanned the crowd, daring to open up his Sight just a bit more than usual, focusing his attention on one person after another, guests and servants alike, looking for the taint of the Witch Lord's magic. The sense of relief he felt when no one triggered his Sight barely offset his frustration that he found nothing to corroborate his instinct's warning.

Then again, the man who tried to shoot the heralds didn't show up to our Sight, either. That didn't make him any less dangerous.

Edvard reported in from his latest circuit, also providing an update on what he had observed of Ridge's situation outside. *"All clear."*

Rett mentally sent Edvard on another patrol, barely stopping himself from tapping his toe or worrying at his lip in annoyance. *Something's not right. I just don't know what.*

He had been on high alert since very early that morning, doing his best to make sure that either he or Edvard watched over the food being prepared in the kitchen to ensure no poison was introduced. The guards did a thorough job of restricting access at the front doors, and Ridge was primed to notice anything amiss at the servants' entrance. Edvard's patrols confirmed that no one had slipped into the upper rooms to make mischief.

A morning reception turned into rounds of smaller meetings, all without incident. The evening meal had been long and sumptuous, as befitted the status of the dignitaries in attendance. These were the ambassadors of the kingdoms that bordered Landria, all of whom sought to improve their trade agreements with each other. They seemed studious to a fault, focused on their goals.

Rett assumed that some of the diplomats were rivals, seeking competing alliances and preferential arrangements. Yet despite that certain tension, no one raised their voices in anger, and he didn't observe anyone whose body language suggested a threat.

As the event neared its conclusion, the group gathered once more in the grand parlor, which was lit bright as day by hundreds of candles in the overhead chandeliers. Kristoph sat on a dais at the front of the room, with the diplomats gathered for final remarks and a toast to all that had been accomplished. Waiters rolled in carts laden with drinks and small cakes for the celebration reception and took up stations all around the room to make sure that none of the guests had long to wait for their desserts.

It occurred to Rett that he had rarely seen the king look so happy and relaxed as if feeling freed from the weight of the Witch Lord's looming threat had brightened Kristoph's outlook, making him look young and full of life.

Only a couple of candlemarks left, and the event would be over. Rett would be glad to have been wrong, already starting to dismiss his fidgeting as the outcome of an overactive imagination.

Something drew his attention upward. He'd barely spared a glance for the ceiling murals when he and Ridge had checked out the room earlier, other than to note that someone had spent a lot of time and money on paintings nobody could admire up close.

With the chandeliers aflame with candles, he could make out the murals in more detail. Several of the panels portrayed stories he recognized from legends and myths of old gods and forest creatures. Others were pastoral scenes, with forests, rivers, waterfalls, and an expanse of clear, blue sky.

Sky. Rett's blood ran cold. *The vision.*

Everything happened at once. He saw the servers bend to do something with their carts, faces blank as if bewitched, lifting the cloth covering to reveal rough barrels...

Gunpowder.

Edvard appeared clearly in his mind, urgency overcoming exhaustion. *"They intend to kill the king!"*

He had no way to signal Ridge, who was outside the mansion. His partner would be too late to do anything even if Rett could raise the alarm. Rett looked back toward the king and saw that one of the carts sat right at the edge of the dais, ready for the monarch to raise the first toast.

"Get out!" Rett shouted above the applause that greeted Kristoph's comments. "You're all in danger! Get out now!"

Rett's heart raced, but everything around him seemed to unfold with dreamlike languor. The audience looked at him as if he were a madman, murmuring among themselves but making no move toward the doors. Rett saw smoke curling from beneath the cart closest to the king and knew the lit fuse gave him only seconds to act.

He launched himself toward Kristoph, running as fast as he could, shoving people out of his way. As he cleared the last few feet, guards belatedly started toward him, but Rett reached the king first.

"Get down!" he yelled, diving for Kristoph as the carts began to explode, one after the other, deafeningly loud. Smoke filled the room as panicked guests screamed in fear and cried out in pain.

Rett's eyes burned, his ears rang, and the blasts shook the room. Bits of plaster rained down from the ceiling.

Kristoph's eyes widened in recognition in the split second before Rett collided with him and sent them both sprawling. There was no cover to be had, just Rett's body stretched protectively over the king's as the nearest cart erupted.

Chunks of the ceiling fell, painted with sections of the mural. This part of the room protruded from the main walls so that there was no upper floor above it. A large piece of plaster and stone fell next to Rett, part of the painting's blue sky, exposing the nighttime vista of stars through the hole in the roof.

Debris pelted his body. Kristoph threw off Rett's protection and began crawling toward the far wall. A hunk of ceiling came down on his head, crushing it like a ripe fruit.

Rett cried out, scrabbling toward the king even though he knew the blow had to have been fatal. He could see only a few feet ahead through the smoke and the choking dust. Sharp fragments tore at his hands and knees.

Something hard struck him on the back of the head, sending Rett sprawling.

I'm going to die here.

Just before he passed out, a dark shape appeared in the smoke, and a force dragged him away. His head hurt too much to think, and his body refused his commands.

Darkness swallowed him before he knew whether he'd been saved or damned.

Chapter Four

The day had been long and boring—and Ridge felt deeply grateful. He didn't believe that the Witch Lord was dead or that Makary stopped wanting to control the throne. But maybe the raid on his hideout had forced Makary deeper underground to regroup. Whether he had ever planned to make a move at Kristoph's summit, the raid might have forced a change in plans.

Excitement meant danger. Ridge had been in the game long enough to value walking away unharmed after an entirely unremarkable day.

He caught sight of Henri once or twice, mingling with the servants, fitting right in. Henri excelled at being useful to the serving staff, who never questioned an extra set of helping hands. Ridge couldn't see Rett, but he knew which rooms his partner would be in, sticking close to the king as his schedule took him from meeting to meeting. He also knew that Edvard provided extra eyes and ears for Rett, patrolling the inside of the manor.

Ridge attached himself to the servants who handled the heavy lifting. He fetched wood for the kitchen, helped to calm a couple of balky carriage horses, and pitched in wherever a bit of muscle was required. Doing so let him move all around the outside of the manor house and keep an eye on who went in and out.

Ridge kept his Sight open, figuring the risk of discovery was worth the possibility of averting a tragedy. He ran into people who were overwhelmed, out of sorts, and downright cantankerous, but no one showed up to him as having been soul-bound to a mage.

Then again, neither had the man who tried to shoot the heralds. Makary and his supporters had plenty of ways to blackmail and intimidate hapless people to their will, without needing freely given consent or wholehearted willingness.

Despite the tedium of the day, Ridge couldn't shake the feeling that something bad was going to happen. His intuition kept him on edge, like a persistent itch under his skin. He tried not to fidget, but he feared the other servants probably figured he'd been chewing on cocoa leaves.

How much can a few dozen old men eat and drink in one day? Ridge wondered as he carried supplies to the kitchen. Servants brought in new wine casks and brandy barrels all day. *If they've had that much to drink, they're either going to get along spectacularly and start singing or break out in a bar brawl.*

Once dinner was over, Ridge started to relax, just a little. He had memorized the king's schedule, and all that remained was a final speech and reception. After everything the diplomats had consumed, carts with yet more delicacies served up a variety of desserts, cheeses, port, and sherry. Then it would be over, they would go their separate ways, and Kristoph's guards would escort him back to the palace.

Maybe, for once, something might go right.

"We don't need more help in the kitchen. Go lend a hand with the horses and get the carriages ready to go." The head butler told Ridge, making a shooing motion toward the stables. He had been the person at the heart of the night's activity, calmly sorting out what needed to be done and who needed to do it.

Tonight, after the guests departed, nearly everything would be packed up and hauled back to the city, along with all but a small crew of retainers who would watch over the shuttered manor house until the next time the king needed it.

Ridge headed for the barn. He liked horses, even the high-tempered ones, and had a knack with them. He certainly felt more patience toward the horses than he did toward most people.

The explosion, even from across the yard, made Ridge's head ring and sent chunks of rock flying, pelting into the side of the barn so hard that pieces embedded into the wood. Horses panicked, nearly trampling people nearby. Smoke billowed from the manor house, and a fine snow of dust fell, making it difficult to breathe and covering everything. Flames roared from the broken clerestory windows of the grand parlor.

The reception. That's where the king is—and Rett.

Ridge plunged a rag into the horse trough and wrung it out, holding it over his mouth and nose as he ran toward the burning building. Servants and functionaries stampeded away from the inferno, jostling him in their terrified rush. He scanned faces, desperately searching for Henri or Rett, but saw no one he recognized, not even any of the other Shadows.

The ceiling collapsed with a crack and rumble that shook the ground, cutting off access from the kitchen side of the building. Ridge circled, fighting his way through screaming, bloodied survivors, soot-streaked and corpse-pale with plaster dust. At the front of the manor, a handful of guards hurried frightened people onto the lawn. From what Ridge had counted beforehand, half the guards had either fled or been inside when the explosion occurred.

From this side, the damage looked even worse. The ceiling had fallen in, flames rose too high for anyone to attempt to enter the ruins of the room, and one stone wall tilted dangerously, likely to collapse at any moment. Ridge ran past the guards, ignoring their shouts, and plunged into the smoke-filled entranceway.

Even with his mask, Ridge knew he wouldn't last long. He could barely see his hand at the end of his outstretched arm, and the air, thick with dust and smoke, burned his lungs and made his eyes tear fiercely. He felt his way down the undamaged wall, needing to see for himself, desperate to know if any chance remained to save Rett and the king.

"Goin' the wrong way!" a man choked as he forced past, shoving Ridge to the side. He looked like a battlefield wraith, covered in blood, eyes wild, skin and clothing charred on one side of his body.

Ridge grabbed the man by his uninjured shoulder and dug his fingers in, holding tight. "Did you see it? Are there survivors?"

"The ceiling fell. Everything's on fire. They're all dead. Everyone...dead." The man wrenched out of Ridge's grasp and staggered down the hallway and out of sight.

Wheezing, Ridge stumbled on, needing to see for himself. The hallway felt like an oven. Fallen beams blocked his path, and flames drove him back, but not before he glimpsed the wreckage.

The entire ceiling was gone, burying those beneath it in the rubble. Fire consumed everything that would burn, sending up a noxious smoke that smelled of burning flesh and hair. Rett would have been toward the far wall, near the king, Ridge thought, in the place the damage was greatest.

If he was near the front, close to Kristoph, then they're both gone.

Ridge turned back, barely able to remain on his feet. He fell to his knees in the entrance hall and crawled the rest of the way to the door, down where the air was cooler and the smoke thinner. Outside, he practically rolled down the steps onto the grass, heaving for breath.

The fire spread quickly along the old timbers, and soon the entire manor blazed, outpacing the efforts of those who threw buckets of water from the well and were quickly driven back by the flames. Ridge stared at the inferno, knowing that between the fallen ceiling and the heat of the fire, no one inside could have survived.

Still, Ridge held out a desperate, doomed hope that perhaps Rett and the king hadn't been at the blast site. *Maybe Rett took Kristoph out a secret passage. Maybe I overlooked Henri in the chaos.*

Ridge searched among the survivors for Rett's face or Henri's familiar profile, but he recognized no one. The servants who had been far enough from the explosion to escape huddled near the stable, soot-streaked, tearful, and shaking. Neither Rett nor Henri were among them, and Ridge found no trace of Burke either. Questioning the servants confirmed that the great hall did not have vaults beneath it, ruling out the possibility of the weight of the collapsed ceiling breaking through to a lower level.

Ridge pitched in where he could lend a hand, helping to calm the panicked horses, then assisting with the grim task of gathering the bodies of those who had been hit by flying debris outside the manor. He kept his ears open, but no one seemed to know anything about the last set of carts to be wheeled inside, the ones that must have carried hidden explosives.

The servants who accompanied the carts were known to the others, long in the king's employ, unlikely participants in a plot to kill the monarch. Ridge had not picked up the taint of the Witch Lord on any of the servants with his Sight, and he knew Rett would have been watching just as closely.

Candlemarks passed before it was safe to approach the wreckage. Ridge joined the men who ventured into the ruined great hall, which was now nothing more than heaped stone and blackened wood. Some of the large beams still glowed with embers that threatened to flare to life given the chance. The smell of charred flesh hung over everything, even when the worst of the smoke cleared.

Most of the corpses they could retrieve had been burned beyond recognition. Some bodies, crushed beneath the weight of heavy stone, couldn't be removed without more manpower and equipment. One thing became painfully clear—there were no survivors.

Ridge tore himself away from the ruins, needing a chance to compose his emotions. His hands were torn and blistered from trying to shovel away the fallen stone, and his face felt burned like he'd toiled under the hot sun. Smoke pained his lungs, and grief constricted his chest. The rawness in his throat coarsened his voice to a low growl. *Rett, Henri, Burke, Kristoph—all gone.*

Now that he had confirmed beyond a reasonable doubt that no one had survived the explosion, Ridge knew he needed to flee before word spread, and an influx of soldiers and officials arrived from the city. If anyone recognized him, questions would arise about why one of the Shadows was present without orders. Burke couldn't vouch for him, and Ridge would make a convenient suspect to blame, providing a way to rush the matter to closure and protect those actually responsible.

He lingered, despite the danger, because leaving meant accepting that the others were beyond hope of saving.

"Hey now, who're you? What're you doing here?" One of the guards strode toward him.

"Just trying to get my breath," Ridge said, which was more truth than lie.

"I've seen you, near the king not too long ago," the guard said. "One of those Shadows, aren't you? What are you doing here? Did you have a hand in this?"

Ridge rose to his feet, fearing the man would start shouting for backup. The guard looked like he'd reached his breaking point, overwhelmed with the horror of the fire and the realization that they'd been betrayed.

"You need to come with me." He reached out for Ridge, and Ridge evaded his grasp. The only way this night could go any worse would be if Ridge had to kill to escape, but he had no intention of being tossed into the dungeon as a convenient suspect.

The guard dove for Ridge and he pivoted, bringing his knee up and his elbow down. The man slumped, lying motionless but still breathing. Ridge glanced around to make sure no one had seen the altercation, then stole the guard's sword and fled into the darkness, intending to put as much distance between himself and Sommerelle as possible.

Ridge spent the remaining candlemarks before dawn in the forest and cleaned up as best he could in a stream, washing the soot, blood, and dust from his skin and hair. He stole clothing off a wash line and tossed his own ruined castoffs into a burn pile. Breakfast amounted to a few raw vegetables taken from a garden and a loaf of bread set on a windowsill to cool, washed down with water from a farm well.

He had a long trek on foot, no matter where he headed. Going back to the safe house wasn't an option since it would require him to take a route likely to cross paths with the soldiers and officials on their way from Caralocia to certify the king's death. The palace city had already been unsafe for Ridge and Rett before Kristoph's murder, and it would be doubly so now.

His head had stopped throbbing, his lungs cleared, and his eyes no longer blurred from the smoke, Ridge considered his choices. None of them were good. If by some miracle, Rett had managed to escape—with or without Kristoph—he would follow protocol and go to their safest bolthole. Henri would do the same.

That gave Ridge a destination, but getting there provided the next challenge. Stealing a horse was a matter of last resort, although it wouldn't be the first time he'd done it. None of the farms he passed had anything except nags for the plow, nothing fit to ride. The irony of being hanged as a horse thief when he was perhaps already wanted for the death of the king did not escape him.

If the Witch Lord is behind this, he's no longer a suspect because he's conveniently "dead." Rett and I earned Makary's ire shutting down his schemes, so we'd make the perfect ones to blame for it. Without Burke or Kristoph, we're at the mercy of the other Shadows, most of whom will be happy to be rid of us since they never liked our way of doing things.

Shit. This just gets worse and worse.

I need to find Kane. He might have learned something when he went back to Sholl that would help us stop the Witch Lord for good. Kane also knows Malachi—and I could use a good mage on my side right about now.

That made a lovely plan, except that Sholl was too far to walk, and it would be too dangerous to show up there so soon after he and Rett had been visible making inquiries. Once Kane heard of Kristoph's death, he'd probably go into hiding as well, since few people truly trusted a spy even under the best circumstances.

Going to Harrowmont was out. If the Witch Lord intended to make Ridge his whipping boy, every soldier in the kingdom could be looking for him. He wouldn't bring that kind of danger to Lady Sally Anne's doorstep. Sheltering runaway women, hedge witches, and mediums—as well as psychic orphans—might evade notice, but no one would turn a blind eye to providing refuge for a supposed traitor.

He wished with all his heart that he could ask Lorella or Edvard whether Rett and the others were really dead. But the risk was just too great.

That left several days of walking to reach their most secret hideaway while trying not to be recognized or attract attention. Ridge took refuge in a farm shed, desperate for a candlemark's sleep. When he woke, he saw a pile of rags in one corner and smiled as a plan formed.

The rags smelled of mildew and mice, but Ridge resolved to make the best of it. One kind of traveler could pass nearly unseen almost anywhere, reviled by all, untouched by cutpurses and soldiers alike. Ridge wound the rags around his face and wrapped them around his hands, covering as much exposed skin as possible.

He hid the sword in the shed—too conspicuous—but helped himself to a couple of butchering knives. Those he concealed under a shapeless coat he found on a peg, and he shoved a squashed hat down on his head to hide his features. For the final touch, he put a dozen nails in a battered tin cup, testing with a jiggle to see how loudly they rattled in lieu of a bell.

Joel Breckenridge, King's Shadow, disappeared beneath the disguise. No one would spare a leper a second glance, save to stay out of his way.

Four days.

Four days of sore feet and rainy downpours.

Of enduring the disdain of the travelers who crossed the road to avoid his path and made a sign of warding as if his supposed illness might be a curse they could catch by merely laying eyes on him.

Four endless days of vigilance, hungry and bone-weary, fearful that every passing rider might somehow see through his disguise and turn him in to the guards.

At least the physical misery of his journey kept him from thinking clearly about the future or feeling the impact of what happened at Sommerelle. Ridge focused on putting one foot in front of the other, keeping body and soul together, foraging for food, and managing a few stolen candlemarks of sleep when his body refused to go on.

When he finally reached the isolated cabin, Ridge couldn't even manage a sigh of relief. Exhausted and heartsick, he just wanted clean clothing, a full belly, and a safe bed.

Still, he took the time to make sure that no one had broken the protections Henri had put on the snug house and that neither thieves nor animals had gotten inside. Satisfied that the refuge remained secure, Ridge found the hidden key, let himself in, and stripped away the filthy rags of his disguise.

For the first time since Sommerelle, Ridge let the awful truth wash over him.

Rett was dead.

Henri too. And King Kristoph.

With Kristoph dead, if Burke survived, he had probably gone into hiding. Kane valued self-preservation above all, so he wouldn't be found unless or until he wanted to find Ridge. Without Kane, there was no way to find Malachi. Which meant that Ridge was on his own.

He slammed down mental walls, locking his heart away, at least for now. Ridge was barely standing. He got the crank on the well working and filled a bucket with water, then took stock of the staples in the cupboards—dried fruit, smoked and salted meat, wheels of cheese, bottles of liquor. Ridge remembered the root cellar and pulled up a trap door to find shelves of crocks full of pickled vegetables, as well as bins of onions, cabbage, and potatoes, plus a couple of barrels each of wine and whiskey. Enough cordwood to last quite a while lay neatly stacked beneath a lean-to not far from the kitchen door.

From the lack of dust, Ridge bet that Henri had been here recently, making his rounds of their hiding places to ensure they were fully stocked. The cabin had a kitchen, a sitting room, and another room large enough for three cots with bedding and trunks to hold their belongings. Shelves in the sitting room had space for a deck of cards, a cup with dice, and a few other diversions. A cache of weapons, enough money to get by for a few months, and clothing to suit every season was stashed in trunks.

As hideouts went, the little house provided privacy, safety, and comfort.

Meant to be shared by the three of them. Not to be the refuge for the last man standing.

He looked out the back window to see several fruit trees, a chicken coop, and a messy garden patch that, despite the weeds, looked like it still had some bounty to offer. A couple of chickens emerged from the brush, and Ridge figured that he would have to chase them to make a meal, but there might be eggs in the coop. An empty fenced area and uninhabited hutch suggested that if he could purchase a couple of goats and rabbits, he wouldn't starve. The pond that glimmered in the distance reminded him that he'd spotted a fishing pole and creel in one corner.

Henri had provisioned for the three of them. Living here by himself, Ridge figured he could get by for several months. Not long enough for it to be safe to return to Caralocia. That would probably never be safe again. Although perhaps the time would be sufficient to get vengeance. For Kristoph. Henri. But most of all, for Rett.

Reality still loomed too large for him to handle when he was hungry and dirty and dead tired. Ridge found a large brass tub and hauled water from the well until a few inches covered the bottom. He scrubbed down, sluicing off mud, sweat, blood, and the rock dust that had gotten everywhere and remained despite his previous attempts to clean up.

He felt human after that, marginally so anyhow. Ridge made a cold supper of cheese, dried meat, and pickles then washed it down with water and whiskey. If he went to the village to get goats and rabbits, he reminded himself to buy bread as well.

Ridge built a fire in the fireplace and stared into the flames. His body was exhausted, his mind overwhelmed, but he still hadn't come down from days of twitchy watchfulness. Maybe the whiskey would help.

There were shelves of whiskey jugs and a couple of casks.

Still not enough.

Not when Ridge was the only one left alive.

He knocked back one shot of whiskey, and then another. He wanted to feel…something. Rage. Sorrow. Maybe the loss was just too big, too fresh.

All he felt was numb.

He had walked away from Sommerelle nearly uninjured. His lungs still burned from the smoke and dust, and small burns peppered his neck and arms where embers fell, but this enemy had been one he couldn't drop with a punch or stop with a knife.

He needed a plan.

Without a plan, either the soldiers would find him and kill him, or Ridge would go after the Witch Lord and get himself killed. The thought didn't bother him nearly as much as it should.

Finally the whiskey hit, taking enough of the edge off of Ridge's ragged nerves to let him slump on the couch, dragged into dreams of fire by exhaustion and alcohol.

He woke with a dry mouth, an unsettled stomach, and a dull ache in his bones matched by the rasp of each breath from smoke-damaged lungs. His head throbbed, less from the whiskey than from the angle of his neck as he slept and from the raw pain in his sinuses. Ridge realized that he had been asleep for most of a day, which was only barely sufficient to make up for what he had gone without.

For three days, he only left his bed to eat and relieve himself. On the fourth day, he dragged himself back to the kitchen, heated water so he could wash, and used a vinegar mix to lighten his dark hair. He had a solid start on a beard and figured it, and the altered hair would help to conceal his identity.

Ridge spent that morning at the table, drinking tea and thinking. Going back to Caralocia would be suicide. Kane might have learned more about the Witch Lord's history on his trip to Sholl, but Ridge had already hit a dead end there, so backtracking would solve nothing.

He needed information before he could set a course of action. Ridge didn't have to use much imagination to know what would be going on at the palace. Kristoph died without an heir, so there would be chaos and jockeying for position among the nobles until a provisional government could be set up and a determination made on how to move forward.

Ridge had no doubt that the Witch Lord would make the most of the opportunity. Makary couldn't show up in person—not without explaining why he wasn't dead, which would inconveniently put him back under suspicion for the murder of the king. Then again, Ridge and Rett always doubted that Makary wanted the throne for himself. The crown made its bearer too much of a target.

No, Makary would be satisfied to be the power behind the throne, getting exactly what he wanted through blackmail, murder, and intimidation while taking none of the risks himself.

Ridge felt certain that whatever ends suited Makary did not bode well for the kingdom itself.

He sighed and looked at the ceiling, drawing in a deep breath. "I know what they say about talking to yourself, but it's too damn quiet in here."

Ridge paced, working through what he knew, putting together the details like they always did when facing a challenge. *Except it's not usually just me doing the thinking—it's all of us, and sometimes Kane and Burke and others too. I don't know if I can do this by myself.*

If I don't, who will?

"Right, then. Let's get down to it." He felt foolish speaking out loud, then realized there was no one to fault him.

"A small group of nobles will preside without the king, and they'll figure out whether there's anyone in the lineage to take the crown," Ridge mused.

"Kristoph's son was stillborn, and the queen died in childbirth. He doesn't have brothers or nephews who are still alive. Cousins, perhaps? That will take time to trace and verify."

He sagged against the wall and scrubbed a hand down his face. "I need information that I don't have. And I won't learn anything by sitting on my ass in this cabin."

As much as Ridge hated inaction, he knew he had to bide his time. Going into town was a risk, not one he wanted to chance too often. He'd need to think of a reason for his sudden appearance in a town where those who weren't just passing through had known each other's families for generations. Something that wouldn't attract attention or be too memorable.

"A peddler. I could have a pack of wares and make a cart for myself with things from the cabin. Not like I actually have to sell them to anyone or go very far. Just make a big circle and come home again."

No, not home. Home was with Rett and Henri. Without them, Ridge was truly an orphan once again.

"Still, not a bad beginning. It'll get me in and out without suspicion. Gives me a reason to show up more than once, after some time passes in between. If I pass one evening every week or so at the tavern, I should hear what's being said," Ridge thought aloud. "Assuming there's anything worth listening to."

He knew that if he was too quick to go into town, it would be for naught since there wouldn't have been enough time for the news to travel. Heralds might not venture to towns this small and unimportant, but people who had heard their proclamations elsewhere would bring that information back, and it would make for lively retelling at the pub. Little enough excitement happened in these farming communities, and the tale of what happened at Sommerelle would be told and retold for weeks to come.

Ridge forced himself to wait. He weeded the garden and harvested the vegetables that hadn't been lost to insects or neglect. Cleaning the chicken coop proved a noxious task, but once he had rid the nests of eggs gone bad and mucked out the droppings, he guessed that the hens and rooster might be worth the bother.

Every morning he trained, sparring with his shadow, throwing knives, pushing himself with hard, physical labor to stay in fighting shape. He worked himself to exhaustion so that with a few fingers of whiskey, sleep came quickly and lasted several candlemarks before the dreams came.

In the first days after he reached the cabin, he dreamed of Sommerelle. Sometimes he relived those awful moments of the explosion and fire, watching the mansion's ceiling collapse, failing to get inside in time to rescue Rett or the king.

Other nights, the dream shifted, and he found himself in their apartment back in Caralocia, sitting down to a hearty meal and a good bottle of wine with Rett and Henri like old times. They chatted and joked as they ate, enjoying the food and camaraderie in those rare days in between assignments when they had the brief but sweet chance to revel in being alive and uninjured before going back into danger.

Sometimes a different dream inserted itself between the memory of times past and the horror of recent days. Fleeting images showed him a dimly lit room and stone walls, and while he couldn't make out other details, the sense of gloom and pervasive despair persisted long after the dream itself ended.

No matter which scenario haunted his sleep, Ridge woke gasping and soaked with sweat, heart thudding, mouth dry. Some nights the dreams came in waves until he gave up and went out to the kitchen, pouring some whiskey and busying himself with dice or cards until he was finally exhausted and drunk enough for dreamless rest.

After the first week, Ridge wondered if the cabin was haunted. He lacked Rett's ability to hear spirits, but he had seen ghosts that were strong enough to manifest themselves. Cold spots appeared and then vanished. He heard the floor creak elsewhere in the house or watched from across the room as a door moved just a bit on its own.

"Edvard?" he called out after he had seen enough to feel assured this wasn't a trick of his imagination.

Long ago, when they were boys at the orphanage together, Ridge and Rett had declared themselves to be brothers and swore that they would fight to the death to save each other. Later, early in their days as assassins, they had sworn on their swords to rescue the other, even if it meant crossing the Shadowed Veil or traveling the Paths of the Damned.

Ridge had taken that vow as seriously as any in his life, and he had failed.

"Edvard, if it's you, please go to Lorella. Tell her what you saw, what you know about Rett. That way I'll know what happened when I can finally return to Harrowmont without bringing damnation down on their heads."

He waited, listening closely. Nothing stirred.

The cabin might be home to a ghost that had nothing to do with assassins or kings, some past resident who died within the walls and did not move on. Ridge would have expected Henri to know if the cabin was haunted, but good safe houses were difficult to find, and trade-offs might have been required.

Ridge swallowed hard. He had not known Edvard when the man was alive, so he had never mourned the ghost's death. For a spirit, Edvard had seemed pretty lively—spying on enemies, carrying messages, and on occasion, manifesting enough to save them in a fight gone wrong. No matter Rett's fate, Ridge doubted that anything would have destroyed Edvard.

But if the ghost wasn't a stranger and wasn't Edvard, then that suggested a possibility Ridge hated to admit. "Rett? Are you—" His voice broke. "Is it you? Is your spirit—"

Ridge listened with his heart in his throat, unsure whether he welcomed silence or wished for certainty and a chance to say goodbye.

Nothing stirred. Moments passed, and Ridge slumped into a chair, defeated.

He knew that the chances of him being able to communicate with Rett as a spirit without help were slim. But he hadn't realized how much he had hoped until no answer came. At some point, Ridge would make it back to Harrowmont and have Lorella channel his partner's spirit. But there was no telling when it might be safe to make that trip or how long Ridge would have to wait.

While fortune tellers and hedge witches remained common despite magic being forbidden, mediums of real talent were rare and much more difficult to find. Ridge couldn't stand the thought of trusting a stranger who might be a fraud. Even if he found a medium of true ability, speaking with Rett would put the psychic in danger and compromise Ridge's safety.

Despite knowing all that, the silence felt deafening, and grief weighed heavy on his heart.

By the time a second week had passed, Ridge found himself looking forward to making the trip to the pub. His beard had grown in, and a hat with a wide brim hid most of his face. Henri had made sure to provide fresh clothing when he stocked the cabin, and what Ridge found looked suitably unremarkable. He just hoped he could truly blend in and that the gossip was worth hearing.

The Iron Bell sat at a crossroads. This area might be far removed from Caralocia and the busy ports, but even out here, travelers still required a hot meal, a stiff drink, and a safe bed for the night. Farmers, merchants, and peddlers made their way along the kingdom's back roads, going from market to market to sell their wares. Once in a great while, a caravan or a troupe of traveling performers might happen by, and their visit would keep conversation buzzing for months.

As pubs went, The Iron Bell was fairly small. Its namesake sat outside on a post, but the clapper had been removed, and the weather had not been kind. The main room held half a dozen tables, a bar with stools along one side, and a stone fireplace at the other. A door behind the bar probably led to the kitchen. Ridge figured that upstairs the pub boasted a dormitory-style room with cots for weary travelers who cared more for a safe bed than for privacy. A barn out back provided shelter for the horses of overnight patrons.

Ridge ambled in around noon, hoping he would find the pub busy with hungry men looking for a quick meal. Two men sat at the bar, nursing tankards of ale over the remains of plowman's lunches. Ridge ordered the same and found a seat close enough to talk if spoken to and near enough to eavesdrop.

"Ain't seen you around," the bartender said, a grizzled man with a gray beard whose broad chest and strong arms suggested he had done plenty of hard work in his life.

"Passing through," Ridge replied over a mouthful of food. "Took a new road this time. For food this good, I think I'll keep this route."

He had been noisy with his entrance, pulling a handcart he made from scraps at the cabin. It held items he could spare, mostly tinware and a few tools, the kinds of things a not-too-prosperous peddler might afford to resell and turn a scant profit. The cart sat outside the pub's main window, so there was no missing it, verification of Ridge's new identity.

"Where're you bound?" The man to Ridge's right spoke this time. He had the hard-worn look of a farmer and smelled faintly of animals. Ridge waited until he had chewed another bite and washed it down with ale before he answered, not wanting to look too eager.

"Here and thereabouts," he replied with a shrug. "Town to town, farm to farm. Everyone can use a pot or a cup or some tools."

"I might have a look when I finish my drink," the man on his left said. He wore a better grade of tunic and didn't smell of the barn. Ridge guessed he might be a shopkeeper. "My wife put a hole in our best pot last week; scrubbed clean through it."

"I get my tin goods from Carrington, up in the far north," Ridge added. "They're made to last." He took another bite of his lunch, hardly a chore since it was surprisingly good. "Just coming back the long way, in fact. Did I miss anything while I've been gone?"

He didn't look up from his meal, as if he expected assurances that nothing much ever changed. When his companions cleared their throats and coughed, Ridge managed a startled expression. "What?"

"The king is dead," the barkeeper replied solemnly.

Ridge let his eyes go wide and hoped he looked properly upset. "No, really? That's not something to joke about."

"Not joking, lad," the farmer said. "Traitors. Betrayed in his own manor. An explosion brought the roof down on him—and killed plenty of others too."

"That's awful," Ridge replied, doing his best to mingle surprise and horror. "Where were his guards?"

The bartender shrugged. "Don't know. They left that part out of the story when they told it."

Ridge shook his head as if it was all too terrible to believe. "Perhaps the story grew with the telling."

"It's the same tale every traveler from the cities has carried," the shopkeeper replied. "And the heralds as well."

"Heralds?" Ridge echoed. "They were here? I mean, I've heard tell of them, but never seen one."

The bartender nodded. "Aye. Just yesterday. Guess they've been sent hither and yon with the news, not that it makes much difference out here, to the likes of us. One king's the same as another, and the taxes always go up."

Ridge turned away, afraid he couldn't hide his grief, real and sharp. Kristoph was someone he had met and served, protected with his life. While Ridge suspected that the unorthodox methods he and Rett used probably gave the king heartburn, Kristoph knew Ridge's face and his name, something remarkable for an orphan boy from a family of no regard.

"But why?" Ridge asked when he could channel his loss into convincing confusion. "Kristoph was a good enough king, as kings go."

"Traitors in his ranks, the heralds said. Two of the King's Shadows," The bartender said, contempt clear in his voice.

"Shadows? The assassins?" the farmer echoed. "Well, what do you expect from hired killers? No loyalty, just sellswords."

Ridge bit his lip hard enough that he tasted blood and willed himself not to stiffen in anger. *They know nothing of the Shadows beyond the name—and tales nursemaids use to frighten misbehaving children. "Be good, or the Shadows will take you."*

"Then I imagine the soldiers have the blackguards in irons." Ridge looked down at his food, although his appetite had fled.

"One of them is dead, burned to a crisp," the other man said, and Ridge fought the urge to be sick. *That's Rett they're talking about.*

Ridge did not need to pretend to make his breath hitch and a lump form in his throat. "And the other?" He could barely force the sound from his throat.

"Always had a partner, the herald said. Guards will find that one soon enough," the barkeeper replied, with the certainty that came with not knowing the details of how things worked. "I don't imagine they'll go easy."

"Drawing and quartering, that's what they do to king killers," the farmer said.

A chill slithered down Ridge's spine. He and Rett were innocent, but they made the logical, most visible suspects when the Witch Lord needed to shift blame. Regular folks had never heard of the Witch Lord, but thanks to the granny tales, nearly everyone knew of the Shadows, even if they only knew a bastardized and twisted version. It didn't matter what the commoners thought. But the idea of the two most unorthodox Shadows being behind the murder would play well with the nobility and those at court, the audience that really mattered to Makary.

If Ridge were captured, he'd get no trial, no mercy. The Council of Nobles would be glad to have an end to the sordid tale, a villain everyone would accept without question. Drawing and quartering would only be a portion of his torment, as they made an example of him to caution others against daring to raise a hand against the king.

If that was to be his fate, then as awful as Rett's death had been in the explosion, he would be spared the worst.

Sard that, Ridge thought. *I'm not going down without a fight.*

"Doesn't really make much never mind out here," the barkeeper said. "But there's chaos in the cities, so they say. Guess that's to be expected, people showing their grief and all. Can't settle anything until they figure out who will wear the crown."

"Might be a problem with that. No heir. Just one baby, born dead. Musta been something of a mule to not make more," the merchant mused.

Ridge tried to hide the way harsh words made him wince. Kristoph was hardly a "friend," but he hated to hear disrespect heaped on a dead man.

And yet, the king's lack of fertility—or that of his queen—posed a problem for the kingdom. Ridge had never bothered to figure out who would succeed Kristoph, but Rett and Henri had bent over genealogy charts for candlemarks, trying to figure out who would be Kristoph's heir.

He felt certain that the Witch Lord knew and had made every effort to either subvert that person or destroy them altogether.

"Guess it's good I wasn't planning on going to Caralocia," Ridge said as if that had been on the peddler's itinerary. "Might let things calm down a bit."

The barkeeper shook his head. "Don't know that things will settle any time soon until there's a new king. Makes me glad I'm all the way out here. All that upset . . . probably get worse before it gets better."

The merchant settled his tab and headed out without stopping to ask about Ridge's wares The farmer took leave of them soon afterward. Ridge nursed his second ale, but no one else walked in, and he didn't want to raise the barkeeper's suspicions.

"Mighty fine lunch," he said as he put his money down on the worn counter. "Ale's not too shabby either. I'll make sure to stop the next time I come this way."

The barkeeper looked up from where he washed tankards in a basin. "A word to the wise—stay off the main roads. There's been trouble."

"Oh?" Ridge did his best not to appear too interested.

"Heard the heralds talking. Ran into brigands, more than once. They're not the only ones to say so, just the latest. A man like you with that cart would be a target."

Ridge appreciated the sentiment behind the warning and nodded. "Thank you. I don't have much choice about traveling, but I'll keep a watchful eye."

He walked back outside, troubled by everything he had heard. Dangerous roads meant keeping his wits about him.

Ridge gripped the handles of the cart and headed down the road, in the opposite direction of the cabin. When he had scouted the route, he'd seen a side road a mile away that would let him double back without risking being seen by anyone in the tavern or risking a visit to town. The men in the pub had given him the information he sought, straight from the heralds. He doubted anyone in town would have more to add, and the less he was seen, the better.

Perhaps others heeded the warnings about brigands because the road was quieter than Ridge expected. He passed a few travelers on horseback who paid him no attention, and another man on foot going in the opposite direction who crossed to the other side to avoid him. That suited Ridge just fine.

When he took the turn onto the side road, Ridge's gut tightened with the sense that something was wrong. No one else was in sight, but up ahead he saw vultures circling, and a dark cloud of flies buzzed and swirled over something in the ditch.

Probably a dead animal, he told himself. *There are wolves in the forest. Maybe they left part of a kill that wasn't picked clean.*

His wariness sharpened as he got closer. Whatever lay dead in the ditch had attracted a lot of attention from the scavengers, too much to be the remains of a small, unlucky animal. The stench of decay put him on high alert, and Ridge pulled his cart to the side of the road and drew his knives.

"Shit." He looked down at the bodies of two heralds. Blood stained their bright red jackets a darker crimson. Both men had been shot. Their horses were nowhere to be seen, and Ridge figured the animals had bolted at the sound of gunfire or been stolen by the killer.

Grimacing, Ridge edged closer, waving his arms to dispel the flies and warn off the vultures that eyed him like fresher meat. He crouched next to the corpses and turned them over. Each had been felled by a single musket shot—one to the head and the other to the heart. Swallowing back bile, he patted down the bodies and removed the packets both men carried that held the proclamations they were to share.

Ridge felt a pang of guilt about relieving the dead men of their money and weapons, but he reminded himself that they no longer had need of them, and he was a fugitive. The glint of metal caught his eye. One of the heralds wore a medallion—the style that Henri's actor friend had given away barely two weeks ago.

Ridge held the bloodstained metal in his hand, overwhelmed by the churn of emotions. The idea of pairing willing spirits with the medallions to serve as a ghostly spy network hadn't done anything to protect these men. It had been a long shot, and now that Rett was gone and Edvard was beyond Ridge's ability to contact, the plan fizzled before it had barely gotten underway.

Still, Ridge took the medallion and slipped it into his pocket. He didn't know if the ghost had fled when the heralds died, but on the off chance the spirit stuck around, Ridge held out hope that perhaps he could eventually find out what happened if he could reach Harrowmont or find a medium he could trust.

Ridge thought about raising a cairn over the dead men, but that would take time, and he did not want to be seen. He retraced his steps to the cart and trudged toward the cabin, casting a regretful glance over his shoulder as the vultures winged back toward their bounty.

When he got home, he stowed the cart and headed inside, feeling the exertion of the long walk in his legs and the heaviness of what he had learned in his heart.

The proclamations carried by the heralds echoed what the barkeeper had told him, announcing that King Kristoph was dead and declaring two of the king's assassins to be the suspects. Ridge didn't know what he had expected to find, perhaps some important tidbit of news, but the reality made bile rise in his throat.

Rett, Henri, and Kristoph deserved better.

Ridge forced himself to eat a cold meal, although he had no appetite. Then he knocked back a couple of glasses of whiskey and let the sorrow wash over him, tearing away his denials and hope.

He had always thought that he and Rett would go down swinging, back to back against impossible odds, wisecracking against fate. Their luck, skill, and audacity had served them well, but he knew, deep inside, that it couldn't last forever. He just hadn't thought he'd be the sole survivor.

The whiskey freed his tears, grief, and rage mingling to sour his stomach and steal away his breath. Scars all over his body attested to the dangers of the job and how often he had been injured. Too many times, perhaps, he had cheated death, recovering from grievous wounds. That made him no stranger to pain.

This felt different. He could deaden the agony of broken ribs or a dislocated shoulder with alcohol and opium. With rest and care, those injuries would heal. But now Ridge felt hollowed out, empty inside but with all the raw edges aflame.

He had felt this kind of pain once before—long, long ago. Those memories were buried down deep, locked away, forgotten until this new grief forced them to the surface. Ridge had been young, but the wound never completely healed, not all the way.

This was how it felt when his family died, leaving him an orphan.

Ridge spent all night drinking and remembering the best times with Rett and Henri, sealing those in his heart.

In the morning, he had a thick head and a foul taste in his mouth. His tears had dried, and the sharp grief had dulled to an ache. In its place, vengeance rose hot, filling the hollowed places with purpose.

Ridge would find the ones responsible for the slaughter at Sommerelle and make them pay. It wouldn't bring Rett and Henri back. It wouldn't clear his name or restore his position. But it would satisfy his need to finish this, and when it was done, Ridge might be able to rest.

If he survived. That part of the plan mattered the least.

CHAPTER FIVE

Rett remembered the crack of the stone and plaster over his head as smoke and dust choked him and flames consumed everything that could burn.

Kristoph lay still beneath him, and Rett felt neither breath nor pulse, but he could clearly smell the blood, and he knew the king was dead.

In the seconds before the breaking of the roof and its collapse, Rett prepared to die. He had known better than to expect a long life when he became one of the King's Shadows. He'd had a good life, full of adventure and purpose, far more than a street urchin could have ever dreamed. More importantly, he'd found a brother in Ridge and a cousin in Henri—family. It was more than enough.

Rett always expected to die fighting shoulder-to-shoulder with Ridge. But now he felt relief that Ridge might survive this. That was the only victory to be won today.

He braced himself to be crushed when the beams broke and the stone fell. Someone—or something—grabbed him by the shoulder. He felt a blow to the back of his head, and then ... darkness.

Rett woke with a throbbing skull and a parched mouth. He could barely move his arms and legs and feared that the knock to his head had damaged him.

Then he realized iron shackles and heavy chains bound him, weighing him down.

Memories eluded Rett, teasing him with snatches of half-recalled images and familiar-but-absent voices. How he'd been injured, who had brought him here, why he was chained—all of that was a blur. He forced himself to concentrate, trying to sift through the jumble in his mind to pick out the pieces that mattered.

My name is Rett.

I have a brother, Ridge.

And someone else close to me, I can't quite recall.

I own a horse.

I was a soldier.

Is that how I came here—wounded in battle and taken prisoner by the enemy?

I think that is ... not quite right ... but close enough.

I know how to fight—if I regain my strength and can break these chains.

As long as I'm alive, I have a chance.

Consciousness ebbed and flowed like the tide, and Rett let it carry him. Someone put water and hard bread within his reach, and he ate when he woke, then slept until his stomach or his bladder roused him.

The gray stone room had no windows, so the only faint light came from the glow of a torch outside the iron bars of Rett's cell.

Dungeon. I've been captured. But I'm alone. Ridge ... he was with me when the sky fell. Where is he now? Is he alive? And did my captors bring down the sky or did I?

Once when he woke, he saw another man sitting in the corner, gray and indistinct.

"Hello?" Rett rasped, his throat scratchy from disuse. The other man looked familiar, but Rett knew it wasn't Ridge, although he couldn't summon Ridge's face to memory right now. This was someone else, and while he couldn't come up with a name, he knew it was a friend.

The image shuddered, blurring around the edges before growing nearly solid once more.

Not a living man. A ghost.

"Can you hear me?" Rett asked quietly. The ghost nodded. "Can I hear you?"

The ghost's lips moved, but Rett heard nothing. Not with his ears and not inside his mind. He felt a stab of disappointment and a feeling of loss.

"Am I supposed to be able to hear you?"

Once more, the ghost nodded. Then the apparition raised one finger to its lips.

A secret? That I can see him? That I used to be able to hear him? Rett accepted the spirit's warning with the odd sense that he was missing something important. He figured that the blow to his head must have addled his brain and wondered if his memories would gradually come back. Rett shifted, and the heavy chains clanked. *I might get better—if I live that long.*

He could think of a dozen questions for the ghost, but asking seemed pointless until Rett regained the ability to hear the answers. Rett listened closely, taking in the sound of his own breathing, the distant shuffle of footsteps, the faint drip of water. His ears seemed to work fine for normal sounds, but whatever ability let him communicate with ghosts was—at least temporarily—a casualty of the accident that sent him here.

But if the ghost could hear him, maybe Rett could still manage to get some answers by sticking to yes/no questions.

"Do you know how I got here?"

The ghost nodded.

"Do you know where I am?"

The ghost paused, then shook his head.

"Do you know who took me?"

No.

Rett shifted until he could sit up with his back to the stone wall, chains clinking as he moved.

"Is Ridge alive?"

This time, the ghost shrugged.

"You followed me here?"

Yes.

Rett had the feeling there was a story behind the simple answer. What mattered right now was that the ghost had a connection to him, and that meant he wasn't alone. Even more importantly, it meant that if Rett could regain his memories, he had an ally, and perhaps together they could figure out a way to escape.

Footsteps sounded, closer now. The ghost winked out, making Rett wonder if he had imagined the whole thing.

"Who were you talking to?" A rough-looking man stood on the other side of the bars. His clothing had a drab, utilitarian look to it but didn't look like a uniform. That stoked Rett's questions about who had taken him and why.

"No one. Just trying to sort out my head," Rett lied, hoping he managed to sound convincing.

The guard stared at him for a moment as if trying to decide if he believed the answer, then rolled his eyes and used a key from a ring on his belt to open the cell door.

"You'll have plenty of time to talk," he said, and a second guard appeared in the doorway, sword drawn, as the first man moved to open the manacles on Rett's wrists and ankles. "Come on." He reached down and pulled Rett to his feet. Rett staggered but managed to stay standing. A shove between his shoulder blades nearly pitched Rett onto his knees, but he kept his balance.

With one guard behind him and another in front, Rett made his way down a torchlit corridor. The air smelled of damp and mildew, but not the heavy stench of filthy bodies he would have expected from a prison.

How do I know what a prison would smell like? Was I a criminal? Where are they taking me? Who wants to talk to me? And what will they do when they find out I can't answer their questions?

The men moved around him, watchful and wary as if he posed a threat. Between his throbbing head and his aching body, Rett would have found that funny if it didn't present both a danger and a protection.

They'll keep their guard up because they think I'm going to try something. That makes it all the harder to actually make a move if I get the chance. On

*the other hand, there's something to be said for being expected to be danger-
ous. Now I just have to keep them from realizing just how weak I am.*

The guards delivered him to a different windowless room.
Unlike his cell, it contained a sturdy wooden chair and lacked a
barred door.

"Sit," the lead guard ordered, giving Rett a shove. Rett stumbled
and caught himself, disoriented and dizzy. He sat, doubting his legs
would have carried him much farther.

Not in the best shape to make an escape.

The guards moved quickly to bind him, securing his wrists
behind him and his ankles to the chair. When they finished, one of
the guards leaned into the hallway and spoke quietly to someone
out of sight of the doorway.

"Ah, good. He's awake." A newcomer joined them, with a second
man in tow. The guards stood out of the way, and the man ordered
them into the hallway with a flick of his hand.

Neither of the strangers had the appearance of guards. Their
clothing was made of finer fabric, and their manner seemed refined,
but the cold glint in their eyes revealed a street cur's ruthlessness.

The first stranger was tall with broad shoulders, in his middle
years. His graying hair and beard were neatly trimmed, slightly soft-
ening angular, hawkish features. He carried himself like a man of
importance, used to being obeyed. Since Rett doubted either man
would reveal their names, he dubbed the leader "Duke."

The second stranger stood a few inches shorter, with a narrower
build. He looked more like a scholar than a soldier, and his clothing, while of good material, lacked the fine cut or finish of the first
man's. Rett named him "Doctor."

When Rett looked at both men, he saw them covered with dark
residue, like something foul had seeped from their pores. That only
hardened his determination to keep them from getting anything of
use from him. Something old and deep within him warned Rett not
to give any indication of what he saw.

"How badly did the ceiling collapse scramble his brain?" Duke
asked.

Doctor advanced warily as if he expected Rett to spring from the chair like a wild beast. Assured of Rett's bonds, Doctor circled him slowly, then stopped to poke and prod at the back of his head. Pain flared behind Rett's eyes, and he lost the contents of his stomach, nearly hitting Doctor's shoes.

"He has a concussion," Doctor said, disgust clear in his tone as he stepped around the puddle of sick on the floor. He tilted Rett's head roughly and forced his lids open, and the glow of the torches flared painfully through slitted eyes.

"He might recover," Doctor said, letting Rett's head drop. "Unless a clot forms in his brain. Does it matter?"

"It would be convenient if he regained his memories before he dies," Duke replied. "He and his partner have caused a great many people a good deal of trouble."

Doctor stepped back, and Duke moved closer. "Why were you and your partner at Sommerelle, when no other Shadows were present?"

Rett looked at him in confusion, knowing what the words themselves meant but not making sense of the sentence itself. "I don't—"

Duke backhanded him, hard enough to snap Rett's head to one side and send up a burst of light behind his eyes. He tasted blood in his mouth.

"I don't remember."

"What of the children with special talents? The ones you stole from their rightful owners?"

Rett stared at him, knowing that an answer would spare him a beating but struggling to think through the fog in his head. He had a flash of memory of a young boy, but it vanished before he could place it. "Children?"

Duke hit him again, a crack to the jaw that reverberated down Rett's spine.

"M'lord," Doctor said. "His head is injured already. Addling his brain more will not serve your cause. There are other places to apply pressure that will not damage his thinking."

That really doesn't sound good.

Duke grabbed Rett by the chin, fingers digging into the bruising flesh. "Where did you hide the children?"

Rett saw a memory of a fortification with high, dark walls, there and gone in his mind. He looked up at Duke, resolved to give him nothing. "What children?"

This time, Duke's fist slammed into Rett's shoulder, knuckles and a large ring driving into muscles that were already painfully sore. Rett gasped but remained otherwise silent.

"Your cause is lost," Duke informed him. "King Kristoph is dead, and so are Burke and Breckenridge. We've made sure you and your partner bear the blame for the king's death. I'm doing you a favor, bringing you here. The penalty for king-killing starts with torture and ends with drawing and quartering. I haven't had to resort to that...yet."

Ridge is dead. That much got through the fog in his mind. *No one is coming to rescue me.*

Rett wasn't sure he was in any shape to be worth rescuing, assuming he left this room alive. But the confirmation of Ridge's death sent a stab of ice through his heart.

I have no reason to survive this. I just hope they aren't able to pry anything out of me that will hurt someone else.

The interrogation continued, a beating interspersed with questions. Rett didn't know the answers and wouldn't have given them if he could. Whoever he'd been when he had his memories, he'd hidden children from monsters and fouled the plans of men like Duke. That bolstered Rett as the blows fell and gave him courage.

Now that he knew he gained no advantage by surviving, Rett had the upper hand. Duke meant to kill him, regardless. Since they both agreed on the outcome, Rett could win by getting to the end sooner than his captor intended, without yielding anything of value. That knowledge filled Rett with cold peace as Duke raged and fists flew.

Now and again, the ghost grew visible in the corner with an expression of deep concern. Rett wasn't altogether sure that the apparition was real, but he appreciated the presence of a silent witness.

If Rett died here—which looked likely—perhaps the spirit could carry his tale to a medium, in case anyone cared to know what became of him.

"If I may make a suggestion, m'lord," Doctor spoke up as Duke finished landing a round of blows across Rett's body. Duke had rolled up his sleeves, but flecks of Rett's blood stained his fine shirt, even so. The man's knuckles were raw, and sweat beaded his brow. Contempt and fury blazed in Duke's eyes, and Rett figured he wouldn't be the first man the noble had killed.

"What?" Duke snapped.

"He's either immune to the pain, or his injury robs his conscious mind of information," Doctor said. "You'll kill him soon and get nothing. Or—"

"Get to the point."

Doctor shrugged. "I can use the flying ointment your witch gave you. That's strong enough to make a man see visions and doubt reality. Using it on the prisoner might access the memories his injuries made him forget. It's worth a try—once he's dead, there's no chance at all."

"Do it."

Rett saw the ghost appear once more in the corner, and he managed a bleary half-smile in acknowledgment, as much as his swollen lips would permit. *Wait for me. I'll join you soon enough.*

Doctor and Duke left the room. One guard entered but kept his distance, remaining by the door as if Rett might suddenly make a break for freedom.

The ghost looked more solid now, and Rett wondered if being closer to death himself allowed him to see the spirit more clearly. Since the guard paid no attention, Rett figured only he could see the apparition.

Why is he here? To help me pass over, or to step in if I weaken and stop me from telling secrets?

Do I know secrets? I must. Duke thinks I do.

Should I lie? No, they'll find out and come back for more.

Maybe I can goad them into going too far. I don't think it would take much to push me past the point of no return. That would solve my problem.

Rett either dozed or slipped in and out of consciousness, rousing at the heavy footfalls as Doctor and Duke returned. Duke had exchanged his blood-stained shirt for a fresh one, unsullied by his role as torturer.

"I'm told this burns like fire in the veins," Doctor said to Rett in a conversational tone, as if discussing the weather. "It works a bit differently on each person. I'm curious to know what it will do to you."

Doctor wore leather gloves and scooped a light green paste from a glass container. The odor made Rett recoil as far as his bonds permitted, and he turned his head, trying not to breathe.

"I want you to tell me what you see," Doctor continued. "Don't censor yourself, no matter how fantastic the images. Beasts, monsters, horrible nightmare creatures. They'll all seem real to you, real enough you'll forget all this. Nothing will exist except the nightmares, and you'll do anything—anything—to make them stop."

He spread the paste on Rett's bare arms and the backs of his hands, then added more on the thin skin of his neck, over the spots where his pulse jumped.

"We're going to ask you questions, and you'll answer. The part of your mind that sees the nightmares will know the answers, even if your waking mind doesn't." Doctor smiled. "You won't refuse us, not once the nightmares start."

Rett felt the sting of the paste grow hotter, sinking into his blood and bone until sweat ran down his face. Breathing already hurt—he suspected he had cracked or broken ribs—but now he panted as the heat blazed beneath his skin.

The room in front of him vanished. Rett found himself running down a darkened street in a city—a bad part of town if the smell and the broken windows were a clue. The road was empty, and his footsteps echoed. He ran for his life, knowing that something fearful was closing on him.

Rett dared a glance over his shoulder and saw a curtain of such solid black advancing that it blotted out the moon and stars. Rett doubled his speed, slipping on garbage, stumbling over the cobblestones, knowing that if that darkness enveloped him that he would be lost forever.

The scene shifted. He bobbed in the ocean, barely keeping his face above the waves, chilled through by the cold. Moonlight revealed a vast horizon, but he was utterly alone. The waves swamped him, and Rett sputtered for breath, only to have his mouth and nose fill again, as quickly as he could clear them.

Body numb, lungs burning, Rett drifted down, and strange creatures swam up, swarming around him. They pulled at him with teeth and pincers, gouging and ripping, loosing a red cloud of his blood to swirl around them as everything grew darker.

"The children. Where did you take the children?"

A voice filtered through as Rett heaved for breath. Again he saw images of a dark fortress, but if he knew the name, it eluded his grasp.

He kept sinking, down below where even the moonlight didn't brighten the surface of the ocean. The frigid water soothed the fire beneath his skin, dulling his pain. His leaden limbs refused to move at his command, keeping him from kicking or striking at the shelled monstrosities nibbling at his flesh and tearing away long strips.

Even the voice grew quieter as if it came from a great distance. Rett gave one final, doomed struggle for air and then relaxed, welcoming the cold dark.

Abruptly, he found himself standing before the gates of the dark fortress he had glimpsed before. This felt different. Nothing hurt, his breath came easily, and his body moved with the strength of a fighter.

The guards at the gates paid no attention when Rett approached them, not even when he walked through the massive doors as if they weren't there. He knew this place, this sanctuary. Yet everything seemed dimmed and colorless, too quiet, empty.

Rett knew it should be different, but he could not think of why. His ghostly visitor appeared beside him, and that lifted Rett's spirits enough to give him the courage to walk up the steps into the keep.

Each room was empty, although nothing appeared out of place. That should have bothered him, but he brushed it aside, moving more quickly as urgency drove him toward a room at the end of the hall, the only light in a gray wash of shadows.

The ghost was close behind him as Rett reached the doorway. A dark-haired woman sat at a table in front of a candle, holding tight to something clutched in her fist.

Lorella.

She looked up, startled. Everything about this place seemed akimbo. Rett knew it was…that place he must not speak of to his captors. The place of safety. For the children.

Rett would die before he'd betray them.

Pretty sure I did just die.

Lorella looked up, startled. Her eyes widened as she realized who she saw.

"You don't have to break it to me. I get it. I'm dead."

"Not completely."

Rett had never been confident around women. He lost his own mother so young, then the monks took him in, then the army, and the Shadows. There were female assassins, but they weren't like mothers and sisters. He didn't know how to read them, what to say.

"We don't have much time." Fortunately, Lorella took control. "If I had to guess, someone gave you flying ointment, not knowing you have a witchy side already."

Rett startled out of old habit. That wasn't something they spoke about. Better not to confess, not to admit. Henri and Lorella knew, but few others.

She licked her lips, nervous. "Edvard brought you here. You scared a ghost. That's not easy to do."

Edvard. Rett knew the moment Lorella mentioned the name that she meant the ghost from the dungeon.

"I scared him?"

"Your captor went too far," Lorella told him. "At the moment, you're dead. If they do the right thing, it won't last. So—gotta be quick about this. Ridge is alive. They lied. Kristoph is dead. Don't know about Burke or Henri—can't say for sure. Ridge thinks you burned with the king, so he's not looking for you. Edvard tried to contact him, but Ridge doesn't have the same abilities you have, and he doesn't have the coin, the one Edvard haunts, which lets him speak in your mind. In your current state, you might have shared glimpses with Ridge in his dreams, but that doesn't mean he'll recognize what he's seen as being through your eyes."

"We need Kane. And Malachi. He's a necromancer. He can help."

A young boy appeared next to Lorella. Rett knew that he was one of the "stolen children" his captor wanted to find, which just reinforced Rett's refusal to give in.

"You don't look good," the boy said.

"Rett's in a lot of trouble, Sofen," Lorella said quietly.

The look in Sofen's eyes seemed far older than his years. "Maybe I can help."

"Ridge won't be able to hear you," Rett said. "He doesn't have those abilities."

Lorella smiled, and Sofen nodded. "We have other ways," she said. "But I don't know if we'll be in time."

Rett swallowed hard, accepting his fate. "That's alright. Just let Ridge know what happened to me. Someone took me when the building fell. I'm in a dungeon. They want to know about the children. I won't tell."

The room had gone hazy as if all the hard lines blurred.

"It's not your day to die," Lorella said with a sad smile. "Good for you."

"Tell Ridge—"

The friendly faces vanished, and Rett found himself back in his body, awash in pain.

"I thought your paste wasn't supposed to kill him."

"He had a bad reaction. It happens."

"He's of no use to me dead."

Rett struggled to follow the conversation between "Duke" and "Doctor." The tether between his soul and body felt loose enough for him to slip the bond again with little effort.

I'm dying.

"He's got a fever. Need to bring that down if you want to have another chance to question him."

"Do it."

Cold water soaked him, then he shivered at the chill. Every movement hurt, and the throbbing in his head never stopped. Guards left him thin gruel and then poured it down his throat when he didn't feed himself. Doctor stopped by to check on him, snapped at the guards, and left.

Rett waited for the fever to finish him. Edvard stayed in the corner, keeping a silent vigil. Rett wished he could hear the ghost in his mind, but between the fever and the headache, even thinking seemed hard.

Ridge is alive, and Lorella will get word to him eventually. At least he'll know what happened. I did my best. It just wasn't enough.

CHAPTER SIX

Days fell into a rhythm of fight training, tending the garden and the livestock, eating, and sleeping. Once a week, Ridge made the trek to the pub, but after the bodies of the heralds were discovered—and their killers endlessly debated—no other news of interest surfaced, and his visits grew less frequent.

He avoided getting to know the townsfolk, aside from those he greeted with a nod at the pub. Ridge made an exception for his neighbor Preston, an old farmer whose land backed up to the plot around the cabin. He shared the bounty of milk and eggs with Preston when the hens and goats produced more than he could use, and Preston brought fresh vegetables from his fields.

They talked about the animals and the weather, companionable but distant. Neither man asked questions that were best not answered. It seemed to Ridge that the older man needed the company. Knowing that it would fall to Preston to find his body stayed Ridge's hand on the darkest of the long nights.

"Someone will need to care for the animals when I go to kill Makary," Ridge told himself. "He'll do right by them."

A month had passed, and Ridge had no more clue of where to find Makary or those responsible for the attack at Sommerelle than he had the night he fled. The merchants who stopped by the pub did not mention the matter after the first weeks, and Ridge grieved how little such things mattered to the regular people of the kingdom. If they spoke of Kristoph at all, it was to wonder who would take the throne and whether the taxes would rise.

Part of Ridge chafed at the inaction when the need for vengeance burned him from within. Yet the repetition and simplicity of weeding and harvesting, milking and gathering eggs cleared his head, giving him time to think. That kept him from charging back to Caralocia on a fatal quest for revenge and absolution.

"The longer I stay away, the more likely it is they stop looking for me," Ridge mused. "I wish I'd had the foresight to fake my death, put them off the trail for good."

Regular people might not care about the crown, but the nobles and functionaries would be embroiled in fights both grand and petty, squabbling for advantage—no doubt one reason a new king had not yet been crowned. The nobles would still want Ridge's blood, want the spectacle of a show trial and a gory public execution, if for no other reason than to lay the matter to rest and bury the guilt of those truly at fault.

Then again, the longer between the king's death and Ridge's return to the city, the greater the likelihood that the attention of both the guards and the Shadows would be taken by more pressing matters. That would afford him a margin of safety when he did go back, and a slim chance was all he asked.

The cabin was too quiet, and Ridge tired of talking to himself, so he spoke to the chickens and the goats, and late in the evening, he carried on one-sided conversations with imaginary versions of Rett and Burke. It might be madness, but there was no one to know or judge.

In a way, the days at the cabin reminded Ridge of the orphanage. The monks who raised them also kept gardens and believed that the hard work helped forge young bodies. He and Rett had both done their turns in the fields and the kitchen, and it surprised him how that early training, long forgotten, came back to his hands and his mind after all this time.

Ridge had been a soldier. Most of soldiering was boredom, broken by frantic periods of terror. This pause allowed him to gather his wits, seek information, make a strategy. If by luck he survived, the cabin would be waiting for him. If not, he'd had a good run.

Ridge had now outlived two families. He would be ready to move on when his quest was finished.

Summer would soon be at an end. Days grew shorter, and nights colder. The long dark would aid him when he returned to Caralocia, providing cover. Whiskey and exhaustion hadn't let him sleep, and he had obsessed over how to hunt down the king's murderers. That left him groggy now, as he stood over a pail peeling vegetables, going through the motions in a daze. Vegetable soup made for a good supper, and it could simmer in the fireplace for the rest of the afternoon without him needing to tend the pot.

Henri had always handled the cooking when the three of them were together. On the road, Ridge and Rett got by on bread, cheese, and dried meat, and sometimes fruit picked from roadside trees. In the past month, Ridge had learned through trial and error to make a few meals that tasted good and filled his belly. Preston made suggestions, and Ridge experimented, deeming the results mostly edible.

A noise near the front of the cabin roused him from his day-dreams, as training and instincts snapped into play.

Ridge changed his grip on the knife, shifting from tool to weapon. He turned, wary and ready to fight.

Outside, a shadow slipped beneath the window. Ridge moved silently into the front room, ready to strike.

The door opened slowly, and a hunched figure crept inside.

Ridge pivoted; knife raised.

"I knew you were alive!"

Ridge froze. "Henri?"

Henri threw off his large hat and dark cloak. "It took me too damn long to get here. But I had to double back and switch roads. For a while, I feared I was being followed. It wouldn't do to lead them to our doorstep."

Ridge pulled Henri into a tight hug and blinked back tears. "I thought you were dead."

Henri hugged him back. "Sorry about that. Couldn't be helped."

Ridge sobered as his smile slipped away. "Rett—"

"He's alive."

Ridge caught his breath. "What?"

"That's why I came to find you," Henri explained, as Ridge shut the door behind him. "As soon as I could confirm it, I came here straightaway. It took me weeks to discover which safe house you chose."

"Tell me everything," Ridge said, breathless. He pulled Henri into the kitchen and put a jug of whiskey in front of him, as well as some bread and cheese.

"I'd been sent by the head butler to the winery some distance away for more barrels," Henri said. "By the time I got back, you were gone."

He took a long drink of whiskey to fortify himself. "I found reasons to linger and help with the cleanup, so I saw what they found when they brought in equipment to lift away the heaviest stones and get to the bodies beneath. There was no doubt about which body was Kristoph. A chunk of the ceiling nearly took his head off. They identified his body by his rings and scraps of clothing. When they pulled out the other corpses at the bottom of the rubble, burned beyond recognition, they said one of them must have been Rett. But it was too short to be him. I knew something was wrong."

Ridge found that he was holding his breath, with a white-knuckled grip on his glass. "Burke?"

Henri shook his head. "Vanished. I would have heard through my sources if he'd been blamed and taken to the dungeons. But there's been no word. Nothing."

Henri took a deep breath. "I went to ground. Figured they'd be watching all of our houses, so I hid among the beggars and pickpockets. I listened and watched. I retrieved a bag of my things one night from one of the apartments, enough to let me change up how I looked when I needed to be someone else."

"Everything we did to save the heralds? It wasn't enough," Henri said with a note of sorrow. "Too many now belong to the Witch Lord. They spread the word that you and Rett plotted to kill the king and carried it out." He snorted. "As if you could have done that alone. But people believed it. They wanted the matter settled."

"How did you find me? Should I pack?" Ridge glanced out the window as if a regiment of soldiers might be on their way to take him back in irons.

"Edvard told me where you were."

"Edvard?" Ridge looked up sharply. "I tried to call out to him. Even did a couple of spells to summon him, but... nothing. Although for a time, I wondered if the cabin was haunted."

"It's a bit complicated. Rett's spirit found Lorella and Sofen at Harrowmont—"

"His spirit? I thought you said he was alive?" Ridge's hope plummeted.

Henri grabbed him by the wrist with an iron grip. "Hold on. I told you it was complicated. Hear me out."

Ridge nodded, but he took another slug of whiskey, just in case.

"One of the Witch Lord's nobles had a man at Sommerelle. He pulled Rett out at the last instant—I never did get the details. Spirited him away to a dungeon and tried to get him to tell where the children like Sofen were. Rett wouldn't say. They tortured him."

Ridge looked down, eyes closed, jaw clenched. "If I'd have been inside with him, I could have saved him."

"That's a load of shit," Henri said sharply. "If you'd have been inside, you'd probably be dead by now or captured with Rett. Do you want to hear the story or not?"

Ridge swallowed hard and nodded, giving Henri leave to go on with a wave of his hand.

"Edvard stuck with Rett. Don't know whether that was because Rett had the coin Edvard haunts or whether Edvard wasn't sure what else to do. Then the person torturing Rett used a witchy poultice when Rett was near death—the combination let his spirit leave his body and go to Harrowmont, to Lorella and Sofen. He told them his story, but then he got pulled back. He didn't die," Henri emphasized.

"So how did you—"

"Sofen and Lorella did what they do. Lorella mobilized the ghosts, and Sofen reached out with visions. A seer found me and gave me Sofen's message, and then a medium passed along the rest from Lorella." A crafty smile lit his features. "Clever, doing it in two parts. Harder for anyone else to get all the pieces."

"And?"

Henri rolled his eyes at Ridge's impatience. "Sofen had a vision of the place Rett's being held. Lady Sally Anne recognized it. Lorella summoned Edvard, who filled in what Rett couldn't. And then Lorella sent ghosts to find Malachi and beg his help. I don't think they'll give up until he agrees."

"You said that Edvard told Lorella what Rett couldn't. Why couldn't he?" Something about Henri's turn of phrase sat wrong with Ridge.

Henri stared into the depths of his whiskey, then took another drink. "Rett got hurt badly when the roof came down. He took a blow to the head that affected his memory. The torture and beatings didn't help." His voice caught, and Ridge understood. "He was able to reach Lorella and Sofen because his spirit was *untethered* from his body. He was dying." Henri looked up and met Ridge's gaze.

"But you said—"

"Rett got pulled back. Lorella thinks that whoever is holding him has someone with magic helping, strong enough to keep body and soul together. That matches Edvard's account as well." He finished his drink and set the glass down heavily.

"If we know where he's being held, then let's go get him." A rescue mission, no matter how bad the odds, beat a suicide vengeance strike.

Henri held his gaze. "Ridge, we need to be prepared. We absolutely need to get him away from those bastards and bring him somewhere safe. But... there's a very good chance that after a month of all he's been through, Rett isn't going to be the Rett we knew. He might never be that way again."

"No!" Ridge slammed his glass down on the table. "I won't accept that. Rett's a fighter. He might have given up if he thought we were both dead, but once he finds out that we aren't, once we rescue him, he'll fight his way through the Veil itself to come back to us."

"Ridge—"

Ridge shook his head. "No. I won't believe anything else. And if he's that … damaged … then dammit, Malachi can fix him. He's a fucking necromancer. And if not Malachi, then the mage of Runed Keep. If that mage is so godsdamned powerful that Kristoph locked him in a warded tower, he can fix Rett. We've given everything for king and kingdom. I'd say we're owed this."

Henri didn't argue, and Ridge figured the other man had decided to let events take their course. He struggled to get his temper under control, and beneath the anger, he wrestled with fear that Henri might be right. *Whatever it takes, we'll fix him. We've just got to get him out alive.*

Henri cleared his throat. "On the whole 'rescue' thing … I have some ideas." He pulled a folded piece of parchment from the inside of his jacket. "Thought this might get us started."

It didn't surprise Ridge that Henri didn't just turn up with news—he had a floorplan and details about the old fortress where Rett was being held prisoner.

"How did you manage to put all this together?" Ridge asked as he made them a late lunch of boiled eggs and bacon that had been cooked slowly over the fire, served with slices of the homemade bread and fresh butter that he'd traded for with Preston.

Henri gave him a wink and a shrug. "Same as always. Connections."

Ridge sighed, but he knew Henri could hear the note of fondness. "Only you could hide with the beggars and suss out how to break into a fortress."

Henri looked up. "You'd be surprised who you find among the beggars. More old soldiers than you'd like to think when they're too busted up to do their jobs. The fort was abandoned years ago, but this fellow had been captain of the guard there. He enjoyed remembering better times, and since it's not being used anymore, he had no qualms about laying it all out for me."

Ridge shook his head. "You're amazing."

Henri grinned. "I know."

They sat down across the table from each other, with a pot of coffee on the hearth to sustain them. Ridge spread Henri's hand-drawn map out between them and studied the floorplan.

"According to George—the former guardsman—Bentham Castle was built four hundred years ago, before King Kristoph's ancestors had eliminated rivals and won the allegiance of the nobles. It saw bitter fighting and survived a siege."

Ridge frowned. "Then why abandon it?"

"I guess the king didn't feel that area needed a garrison," Henri replied. "George didn't know—it was after his time. But not actually so long ago, perhaps ten years. In this case, I don't think 'abandoned' is the same as 'ruins.' I think it just means the garrison withdrew and locked the door behind them."

"Great. So it's a functioning fortress—that's been taken over by one of the Witch Lord's loyalists," Ridge muttered.

"Want to bet whoever took it over didn't bring an entire garrison?" Henri replied. "For one thing, most of the nobles don't have that large a force. Not to mention that someone might notice an army marching cross-country. A few carriages, on the other hand, wouldn't attract attention."

"If the fortress still belongs to the crown, doesn't anyone official check on it?"

Henri shrugged. "My guess would be not often. Why would they? And it may 'belong' to the king in the same general way everything in the kingdom 'belongs' to him. More likely, it belonged to a noble family who built it to defend the lands given to them by the king, and as long as their interests lined up with those of the crown, the issue of who owned it was just a matter of wording."

"Who built the fortress?"

"According to George, the builder was the Duke of Letwick," Henri replied. "Which sounds possible. Letwick was one of the last to swear allegiance to the House of Braedon—Kristoph's family line."

Ridge had stopped trying to find out a long time ago why a man with Henri's intelligence and skills had begged to be taken in by a couple of assassins and serve as their valet. He figured Henri had his reasons. That didn't stop him from wondering.

"What kept Letwick from supporting Kristoph's ancestor?"

"I imagine he wanted the throne for himself," Henri replied.

Centuries-old squabbles seemed far removed from a kingdom in crisis and a Witch Lord out to cause chaos. Ridge and Henri hunched over the floorplans as the sun moved across the sky, debating the best angle of approach and where they might find a weak point to defeat the fortress's defenses.

"If this is truly one of the Witch Lord's loyalists hiding with a small number of guards, then they can't keep watch effectively," Ridge pointed out, sitting back and crossing his arms over his chest. "It's too big for there to have only been one or two men on guard duty at all times back when it was in use, plus they would have also had someone at the gate or patrolling the perimeter."

He shook his head. "A noble might bring a dozen guards or so. Most don't have a large number of their own soldiers to begin with, and they'll have to leave some behind for their main holdings. That's a mighty big fortress for not many men, especially since they'd be likely to keep shifts, which means even fewer guards awake at any one time."

Henri nodded. "Unless they're keeping multiple prisoners, I doubt that whoever is behind this needs that many guards. And we can be pretty sure it isn't the Witch Lord himself. Makary has everyone believing he's dead—which is very convenient for him. He's not going to tip his hand by doing any of the dirty work himself. When we go after Rett, don't expect to bag the Witch Lord as a bonus."

Ridge shook his head. "No, I didn't think we would. He'll stay hidden until more time has passed after Kristoph's death. He doesn't want the crown himself—he just wants a figurehead who'll do his bidding."

Henri rubbed his eyes. "I get tired of all this sneaking around. At least when someone rides in with an army at their back, everyone recognizes the enemy."

Ridge leaned forward again, squinting at the plans. "With only a small force at the fort, we can't slip in among the garrison and get lost in the crowd. So going through the gate isn't going to work. That leaves us going over or under."

"Or both," Henri said, looking up to meet his gaze. "I know that on a good day, the two of you can scamper up and down a rock wall like squirrels. But we have to get Rett out, and he's not going to be in any shape to climb. If it's all the same to you, I'd rather not plan to blow up the portcullis."

Ridge managed a lopsided grin. "You're no fun."

"That's why I'm planning to go in here," Henri said, pointing to a place on the backside of the fortress. "There's a passageway that was originally a storm drain, but at some point, it got enlarged to also be a way to escape if the soldiers ever faced an unwinnable assault."

"Wouldn't it be blocked off?"

Henri shrugged. "George didn't think so. The tunnel was a secret—they didn't want soldiers sneaking out, or bringing in smuggled items or 'companions.' He only knew because he was captain of the guard."

"So the people who are holding Rett might have no idea, especially if they were never stationed at the fort when it was active," Ridge mused.

"Or weren't senior enough to be privy to the secret. Right now, we've got no idea whether they've got any connection to the Letwick family or just found a convenient, vacant site that made a good illegal prison," Henri said.

"Here's where I wish one of us could hear ghosts and that we had Edvard back with us," Henri grumbled. "We could send him in to do some reconnaissance. As it is, we're going to have to guess where they're keeping Rett and assume that the tunnel is still functional—and that could cost us time if we're wrong."

"As far as figuring out where they're keeping Rett, his captors have the run of the whole place," Ridge pointed out. "So they don't need to worry about hiding from anyone. They'll do what's easy and take him to the stockade. It's set up to keep someone imprisoned, and there's probably a place for interrogation."

His jaw tightened at the word. Bad enough that Rett had been kidnapped and locked in a dungeon, but the thought of torture made Ridge's worry turn to sheer fury.

Henri watched him with a knowing expression. "You're thinking that you want to get revenge," the man said. "You're positively chafing for it."

"They killed the king. And what they've done to Rett—"

"I care more about Rett than any king," Henri said. "My loyalty isn't to the crown—it's to the two of you. Even though there isn't a whole garrison at the fort, we're still going to be outnumbered, and Rett won't be able to help fight our way out. I know you don't like the idea of running away without settling the score, but we'll just get ourselves—and Rett—killed if we try to take them all down with us."

Ridge looked away and growled in frustration. Henri went to the kitchen and brought back bowls for the soup and a ladle for the pot, while Ridge carefully moved the map of the fortress so they could eat. He knew Henri was right, but he didn't have to like it. Ridge much preferred action. Now that the chance to deliver some much-deserved vengeance presented itself, part of Ridge paced like a wild thing in his mind, eager to get started.

Henri put a bowl of the hearty soup down in front of Ridge and handed him a spoon. He bustled around the kitchen, clearly remembering where he had stocked provisions, and taking in stride the fresh additions Ridge had added to the larder from the garden and his trade with Farmer Preston.

"Didn't figure you for a country boy," Henri said as he returned with the bread and butter. "I would have liked seeing you chase down those chickens." He chuckled, and Ridge rolled his eyes, grateful for the break in the serious conversation.

"You probably could have charged admission," Ridge admitted. "Got my arms pecked something awful for my trouble too. The damn goats kicked me in the shins, and one of the rabbits bit me."

"Looks like you settled in pretty good," Henri said, looking around the cabin. "You even cleaned up the vegetable patch."

Ridge looked toward the fire, remembering the turmoil of those first days. "I had to keep busy, or I would have lost my mind," he confessed. "I thought you and Rett were dead. No one could find Burke... then the heralds were murdered. Everyone I cared about was gone, and everything we'd risked our lives to do meant nothing. The animals, the garden, cooking—it kept me from charging back to Caralocia to take as many sons of bitches down with me as I could."

Henri gave him a measured look. "I'm glad you didn't do that. Because Rett would kick your ass—in this life, or the next. And I've got no desire to find a new household. They'd all be boring compared to the two of you." He kept his tone gruff, but Ridge clearly heard the concern and affection in Henri's tone.

"Yeah, well, I need to stay alive to be a pain in the ass for Burke if he shows up. He'd miss me if I were gone."

"Keep telling yourself that," Henri wisecracked, although they both knew there was a hint of truth in the comment. Ridge and Rett complicated the Shadow Master's existence, but his forbearance suggested he valued their results. Ridge suspected Burke even found their adventures to be amusing, although the other man would never admit it.

The soup turned out better than Ridge had dared to expect. Henri kept him entertained with tales of odd or amusing incidents from the past month and avoided mentioning the fear of discovery and his worry for Ridge and Rett.

Ridge returned the favor by regaling Henri with more stories of his misadventures as a would-be farmer and how Preston had finally taken pity on him. Together they finished off the loaf of bread and emptied the kettle of soup, ending with some cheese and whiskey.

"You're right," Ridge said, without looking Henri in the eye. "About the fortress. Rett has to be the focus. I just... really want to take the last month out on some deserving bastard's hide."

Henri chuckled. "If you weren't an excellent predator, you wouldn't be a damn fine assassin. I didn't figure that you were holed up writing mournful ballads for the bards."

Ridge shivered. "Perish the thought."

"You'll get your chance." Henri's voice dropped to a growl. "I'll be right there to help you blow the whole fucking nest of vipers straight to the abyss. After we save Rett."

Ridge knew what Henri wasn't saying out loud. They might end up taking vengeance on Rett's behalf—but without his help—if the damage inflicted couldn't be healed. Or if they arrived too late.

CHAPTER SEVEN

R ett groaned, rolled over, and lost the meager contents of his stomach. His body ached, his head throbbed, and he felt like he was burning from the inside.

No one responded to the noise, and Rett fell back, exhausted.

It registered that he lay on a cot instead of the cold stone floor and that he had managed to retch over the side of the bed. Maybe his almost-death had worried his captors, if they dragged a rickety cot into his cell. Only one ankle was manacled—an improvement of sorts. He felt too weak to get out of bed, let alone make a run for it.

His memories were a jumbled mess, even before Doctor had nearly killed him with whatever magicked paste had been smeared onto his skin.

He struggled to determine whether the snatches he recalled were dreams, memories, visions, or hallucinations. All felt vivid, but they weren't equally real.

Does it matter? I'm going to die here.

Rett glanced toward the corner of the cell. Edvard sat with his knees drawn up, watching him worriedly. "It's alright," Rett said quietly enough so that the guards wouldn't wonder. "You don't have to stay all the way over there."

Edvard unfolded himself but didn't come closer. The longer Rett was awake, the more the blur of memories sorted themselves, although he wasn't sure he could trust his senses or his recollections.

I remember being beaten. Rett recalled Duke's anger and the sound of the other man's fist connecting with his face and body, the snap of bone, and the slap of flesh. Rett's tongue slipped over his lips and

100

tasted dried blood. He felt bruised all over, and one eye was swollen partway shut.

And yet, as he gingerly tried to move his limbs and shift his torso, nothing seemed broken. He had been certain that had been the case. He hurt all over, but while he hadn't been completely healed, it didn't hurt to breathe.

They've probably healed me just enough to keep me from dying, so they can have another go at me.

Rett stared at the stone ceiling, trying to sort facts from imagination. He'd grant that Edvard was real. The ghost seemed to expect Rett to hear him, and since he couldn't, Rett chalked that up to his injuries and whatever potions Doctor gave him to keep him drugged.

He remembered flashes of red, a man's scream, and the sound of a matchlock firing. Two men dressed in heralds' uniforms fell from their horses and lay still, eyes staring. Their frightened mounts galloped off.

Vision, he thought, since Rett felt reasonably certain he hadn't witnessed the shooting himself.

He remembered being overtaken with smoke and dust, hearing men screaming as flames rose in the wreckage. Chunks of stone pelted him. The king's body lay within reach, head caved in from a large piece of the ceiling.

Memory, Rett thought. *That was real.*

Rett saw himself running across rooftops with Ridge just a few steps behind, carrying a child. They leaped from roof to roof to escape pursuers, something they had done a hundred times. But Ridge's footing slipped, or perhaps a thrown blade caught him, because he wavered on the edge, eyes wide with terror as the child on his back scrabbled to keep hold. Ridge met Rett's panicked gaze, swayed, and fell back, turning and flailing until he and the child hit the cobblestones with a sick thud.

Rett's heart raced, and his breathing grew fast and shallow. *Nightmare. I remember that—we got away safely. But I dreamed for a week of what might have gone wrong.*

The next image tested him. Rett recalled being at Harrowmont, pleading for help from Lorella and Sofen. Begging them to let Ridge know what happened to him.

The memory had the weight of reality without the distortion of dreams. *But that's not possible. I'm leagues away from Harrowmont, and to talk to Lorella, I'd need to be a ghost.*

Oh.

Rett remembered the white-hot pain as the paste Doctor applied made him feel like he'd been flayed alive. *Flying ointment,* a voice from the recesses of his brain supplied. He'd read about it somewhere, a mixture of deadly plants that produced vivid hallucinations. But for those truly gifted, the lore suggested that the paste could allow a witch to dream walk, or a seer's spirit to leave his body and travel the paths of the Veil.

Is that what I did? Lorella could see me because I wasn't completely alive. Sofen could hear me because I wasn't completely dead.

He struggled to remember the details and wondered just how close to death he had been.

She told me that Ridge was alive. Gods above, I hope that part is true! It's too late for me, but at least if she can get a message to Ridge, he'll know what happened. That's better than him always wondering. Best I can do.

Gods, I don't want him to get caught trying to rescue me. I'm done. Maybe Henri survived too. Even if Ridge can't be a Shadow, he's alive and free.

I'm just sorry I'm leaving him on his own.

A tremor worked its way up Rett's body as chills alternated with fever. Someone had come in while he was asleep or unconscious and left him food and drink. The water by his bedside tasted of willow bark, meant to bring down his temperature. He eyed the bread and cheese with distaste, doubting it would stay down better than the last.

I wonder where they're keeping me. It's quiet—too quiet. Not the dungeon under the palace in Caralocia. Where am I?

Does it matter? I'm not going to survive, and Ridge won't get here in time if he even knows where to look. Edvard is with me. I won't die alone

I couldn't have asked for a better partner, friend, or "brother" than Ridge. I hope he knows that.

Fever drenched him in sweat; chills had him shaking until he thought his teeth would break from chattering. Rett's stomach clenched, but he had nothing left to expel. He curled up into a ball on his cot, arms wrapped around himself, knees drawn into his chest.

The cell around him dimmed. When Rett opened his eyes, he found himself somewhere else entirely, somewhere he felt certain that he had never been.

The library shelves stretched from floor to ceiling, filled with leather-bound manuscripts and rolled parchments, and the air smelled of ink and candle smoke. The room held two sturdy wooden tables, each with four chairs. A lantern sat on one table, where a book lay open as if the reader had just stepped away. Next to the book was a piece of parchment, a quill pen, and an inkwell.

A university, perhaps? Or a mage collegium?

When Rett looked to his left, he saw that the room extended into shadows farther than he could see. Shelves of books stretched into the distance, a scholar's dream.

A man emerged from the corridor, carrying a thick tome. He had a solid build, medium height, with red hair, and a russet beard. He didn't notice Rett right away, then looked up with surprise.

"You startled me." His eyes narrowed. "I don't remember seeing you before. We don't get many new people."

"I just got here," Rett said, still not sure where he was. Figuring it was a vivid dream, he decided to play along since he had nothing better to do. "I'm Rett."

"Brother Tom," the stranger replied, and Rett realized that the other man wore a monk's cassock. Rett was about to come up with an explanation for why he wasn't in similar garb, then he glanced down and saw that his dream had helpfully changed his clothing to match.

"This is a good library for studying the old books," Tom said, returning to his place at the table. "There aren't many of us, but we do important work—copying old manuscripts, cataloging the archive, researching topics when the need arises."

Rett nodded. "I'm good at research," he said, still trying to figure out where he was and how he got there. *This can't be real. Or at least, if the place is real, I don't think my body left the cell. So what happened? He can see and hear me, and he doesn't act like I'm a ghost.*

"I haven't had the full tour yet," Rett said, walking slowly along the bookshelves and appreciating the rare works included. The monks at the orphanage had made sure that all of their charges could read and write, and those who showed promise found jobs as scribes and archivists. Rett had been good enough to learn plenty of useful skills but not quite excellent enough to risk being claimed by the priests.

"I don't know what you're used to, but Green Knoll is small and cozy, as archives go," Tom said. "Everyone's friendly, the food is good, and the beer we brew is amazing." He smiled, no longer wary now, accepting that Rett belonged.

"That's good to know," Rett replied. "I'm sure I'll like it here." He had no idea how long he would be able to stay, but he was in no hurry to leave.

"I don't want to keep you if you're supposed to be somewhere else," Tom said as if he were truly concerned that Rett might have wandered off, not like he was trying to get rid of him.

"They dropped me off here and said to get acquainted with the collection," Rett lied. "But I don't want to hold up your work."

Tom chuckled and shook his head. "You aren't. And it's not like I'm going anywhere. Green Knoll is completely self-sufficient. Farm, dairy, brewery—we never have to leave. It's a lot of work for just a few people, but it's peaceful. Safe."

A bell in the distance tolled. Tom closed his book and stood. "Time to get ready for dinner. Maybe tomorrow, if they don't assign you to something else, you could come and help me with my research."

Rett smiled. "I'd like that."

Tom took the lantern and headed into the hallway, with Rett following him down a stone-walled corridor.

Rett never reached the dining area. Brother Tom and the monastery vanished, and Rett found himself back on the cot in his cell, tossing and turning with fever.

Rett didn't know how much time passed, but when he woke, both Duke and Doctor stood inside his windowless room.

"We need to find out what he knows. We're wasting time." Duke sounded angry.

"If you want answers, you need to let him recover," Doctor snapped. "He had a very odd reaction to the ointment. Unless you're in a hurry to kill him, and then you might as well just slit his throat."

"I want the names of his co-conspirators. We knew he was working with others aside from his partner. Locations. And I want to find out where he hid those godsdamned children!" Duke roared.

"He's likely to remember all those things much better once his fever goes down the rest of the way and his concussion heals—unless you keep punching him in the head."

"Just fix him. I'll be required to give a report, and I don't intend to go empty handed," Duke replied, in a tone that made it clear Doctor would face the consequences if that were to happen.

Rett heard Duke stomp out of the room. Doctor muttered under his breath, imprecations that gave Rett to know that while the two men were cooperating for now, differences between them ran deep.

"You've caused me quite a bit of trouble," Doctor said to Rett as he came closer. Rett didn't open his eyes, but he felt the man sit on the edge of the cot next to him and then begin to wipe down his face, arms, and chest with cool water from a bucket.

"I'd really rather not be here," Doctor went on. "Only I wasn't given a choice. So the sooner you tell us what you know, the sooner I can go home, and you can move on."

Rett doubted that he still knew anything of value. His sluggish thoughts and confused memories offered a stew of nightmares. He could only hope that the fever killed him before Duke deemed him well enough for further interrogation.

Doctor forced Rett to swallow warm broth and tepid water, threatening to allow him to drown in his own vomit if he dared bring the liquid back up. When he finally felt assured Rett wasn't likely to puke, Doctor stood up.

"You had a most interesting reaction to the ointment," he said. "I think you're sensitive to magic—or that you've got some dark ability you've kept hidden. I intend to find out why you reacted the way you did. Perhaps a smaller dose will create the desired effect."

Rett's heart froze at the words. His foggy memory supplied that he and Ridge had been careful to hide their Sight. Being found out no longer mattered to Rett since he would soon be beyond consequences. But he did not want anything Duke or Doctor learned to put Ridge in danger.

Doctor kept talking, but Rett slipped in and out of consciousness, and sometimes he slept. Either the nightmares did not plague him, or he fell into too deep a sleep to care. Nothing felt like when his spirit traveled to see his friends, and Rett hoped that didn't happen again, because he feared Doctor might find a way of following him and revealing their hiding place.

Instead, he found himself back at Green Knoll, in the monastery. Rett wasn't going to complain. Of all the places his damaged mind might take him, this was by far one of the best.

Rett had heard stories all his life about where people went when they died. He'd always thought most of the ideas were too fantastic to believe. But he rather liked the notion of his consciousness returning to its happiest memories, reliving them until finally fading away.

Since he felt certain that he had never even been to Green Knoll before, let alone having happy memories of it, Rett was at a loss to understand when he found himself at the library door just as Tom looked up from his work.

"Oh, there you are. I missed you at dinner last night."

"I, um, didn't feel well. I think the travel upset my stomach."

Tom nodded sympathetically. "I hope Brother Alson shared some of our mint tea with you. It's very good for stomach ailments."

"I'll make sure to ask," Rett replied. He came around to the other side of the table, and when Tom didn't shoo him away, Rett sat across from the monk.

"What are you working on—if it's alright to ask. I can probably be of help."

Tom slid the books around so Rett could see them. "I just finished reconciling the accounts of the Fifty Years' War. There were a lot of conflicting descriptions—not surprising considering people from both sides wrote their stories, and people had different vantage points. I certainly wasn't able to eliminate all irregularities. But I was able to trace the origins of certain recurring descriptions and match them to contemporary accounts."

He smiled. "No one outside these walls will care, except for a historian or two, but I'm quite pleased with the results."

"How long did it take you?"

Tom thought for a moment. "Ten years."

"That's impressive," Rett said. He knew the value of reliable history when it came to the kind of research he and Ridge did on some of their assignments. That sent a pang of loss through him, and he looked down.

"Are you alright?" Tom asked, worried. "If it's your stomach again—"

Rett shook his head. "No. I'll be fine. I just recently lost people close to me, and sometimes a stray thought brings up memories."

Tom nodded with a grave expression. "Ah. I'm sorry for your loss. Is that what brought you to Green Knoll?"

"Indirectly," Rett replied, being as truthful as he dared. "I'm glad to be here. Seems like a nice place."

Tom regarded him for a moment. "I think you'll fit in well here. It takes a certain type. Probably why there are so few of us. Nothing exciting ever happens. We all get along. Not everyone is cut out for that. We're not the place for anyone dramatic."

Rett smiled sadly. "I've had more than my fill of drama. It's overrated."

He had yet to glimpse any of the other monks, and Rett preferred it that way. He wasn't sure whether his imagination brought him here to find the peace Tom described or if some combination of his magic and the ointment opened a door in his mind to somewhere else. Rett liked Tom, and he had no desire to meet the other monks, in case they would not accept him as easily.

He wasn't even sure the other monks could *see* him.

Maybe I'm the ghost haunting his library. I guess there are worse places to spend the afterlife.

"How did you decide to become a monk?" Rett blurted, and Tom looked up, surprised but not angry at the interruption.

"I was an orphan, and they took me in when I was little," Tom replied. "Not here—at another monastery. Time passed, I grew up, and I realized I wanted to stay. We came to Green Knoll when I was fifteen or so. I imagine we'll all be here until we die."

Tom spoke with such certain contentment that it made Rett long for what he had lost. Not the constant danger or the blood and death; he missed the quiet evenings between assignments at one house or another, drinking and playing cards with Ridge and Henri.

"You're lucky," Rett said, trying to keep the edge out of his voice.

Tom nodded. "Yes, we are."

Once again, the peal of the bells interrupted their conversation. Tom set his work aside. "Lunchtime," he said. "I hope you'll join us. it's not good to go hungry, and Brother Randall's bread is the best I've ever eaten."

"I'll be along in a minute," Rett told him. "Which way to the garderobe from here?"

Tom gave him directions in the hallway and promised to save him a seat. Rett headed off in the opposite direction, trying to figure out another excuse not to join the group—assuming he didn't vanish like the last time.

He nearly ran into the tall, white-haired man who came around the corner. They both recoiled from the near-miss, staring at each other.

"Who are you?" the older man hissed. "You shouldn't be here."

Rett woke, chilled and shivering, on his cot in his cell. He felt slightly better thanks to the water and broth, but making any sort of recovery filled him with dread. Recovering meant a return to torture and interrogation.

Maybe, if I'm lucky, Doctor will mistake the dose of his ointment again, and this time it will stop my heart.

CHAPTER EIGHT

"Now all we need are horses." Ridge packed weapons from the stash Henri had hidden when he provisioned the cabin. He grinned when he found a grappling hook, rope, and plenty of throwing knives.

"Already taken care of," Henri assured him, looking up from where he assembled supplies to tend Rett's wounds. Ridge figured Henri had probably brought some of the more potent and less legal potions with him from the city, to add to the cache of useful items he had stashed in the cabin. Given their job, keeping doctoring supplies on hand was essential.

"So where are these horses?" Ridge asked, glancing out the window.

"Stabled about a candlemark's walk from here, under a different name. Got us three nice horses—strong and fast—plus saddles and tack. Paid the boarding six months in advance, in case we have to hole up here afterward."

"You're amazing, as always," Ridge replied with a grin

Henri cleared his throat, a sure sign that he expected Ridge to react badly to his next words. "I was thinking we'd only take two of the horses."

Ridge's smile faded. "What about Rett?"

Henri met his gaze with a sympathetic expression. "I doubt he'll be able to ride alone, Ridge. Especially if we have to make a run for it."

Ridge caught his breath. Now that they were preparing for the mission, it forced him to face the details. He and Rett had ridden out of plenty of bad situations, covered in blood and barely conscious. The idea that Rett might not be able to sit his horse settled like a lump of ice in his stomach.

"Think about it," Henri said, gently arguing his point even though Ridge hadn't spoken. "It's not his usual horse. Unfamiliar territory. And we don't know how badly he's hurt. If we've got to ride for our lives, we sure don't want him falling behind."

Ridge swallowed hard and ducked his head, then nodded. "No—you're right. He can ride with me. We've done it before. Just haven't had to do it more than once or twice."

Ridge knew how frightened Henri was for Rett—sympathy was clear in his eyes. Ridge felt certain that Henri was equally worried.

"Like I said, the stable's been paid in advance, we'll just say we'll be back for the other horse and not say exactly when." Henri shifted his attention to the bag he was busy packing, giving Ridge a chance to compose himself.

"Preston said he'd take care of the animals," Ridge said, surprised when he realized that he might miss those damn chickens. He resolved not to tell Henri that he'd named them, as well as the goats and the rabbits. "Told him he could have the eggs and anything out of the garden that needs to be picked. No reason to let it go to waste."

Henri gave him a look. "I think you actually like it here."

Ridge shrugged, irritated that his friend could see through him so easily. "Yeah, it kinda grew on me. I'd like to come back here sometime." *If Rett and I can't go back to being Shadows, this isn't so bad. The three of us, chasing chickens. Good place for Rett to recuperate. Quiet.*

He didn't let himself think about the scenario where Rett didn't fully recover and needed a quiet place to die.

"See how things go," Henri said. "It's paid up—and it'll be here when we need it again."

Ridge felt a surge of gratitude at Henri's tact, although he knew the other man had also surely figured out the worst-case scenario.

"There's no way to get to Bentham Castle any faster?" he asked as they locked the cabin and headed for the stable.

"I bought us the best horses I could find, but we don't know how they're going to handle or how long they can go at a time. Lame one of them, and we've got big problems," Henri replied. "Not to mention how riding past everyone like our tails are on fire is a sure way to attract attention we don't need."

Ridge had figured as much, but he still had to ask. Now that he knew Rett's situation, he hated any delay. "We're going north, away from the larger cities. There's not a lot out here except farms and sheep."

Landria's capital and its bigger cities clustered near the coast, and so did the majority of artisans and tradespeople who made goods for export. Merchants and caravans brought goods out to the rural areas, and farmers hauled their produce and livestock to markets that supplied the cities. This far from the coast, most people made do with the food and goods that could be produced locally. That meant the roads that led even farther north from here were likely to be quiet, with little traffic.

"We can hope," Henri replied. "Of course, it makes it hard to blend in if we're the only ones on the road."

Their cover story, in case anyone bothered to ask, was a variation of Ridge's peddler persona. They brought a variety of items they could do without in bags they intended to discard once they reached the castle, since passing themselves off as merchants would be the least of their concerns on the return trip.

"Do you think they've sent the Shadows looking for me?" Ridge asked after they had ridden in silence for a while. He and Rett retained their positions at Burke's discretion, despite the open loathing many of their fellow assassins felt for them. Without Burke, they had one sure ally, Caralin, and a few others who might turn a blind eye or pass along information.

In a fight, they were largely on their own.

"I wouldn't be surprised," Henri said. "If Burke went to ground, who would be giving orders?"

"Finley," Ridge replied, with a curl of his lip. "Guess I have my answer."

Assassins were drawn from the army, recruiting those who excelled with weapons, infiltration, city fighting, and hand-to-hand combat. Some, like Ridge and Rett, had been penniless orphans, from the bottom of Landria's society. Others, like Finley and Burke, came from aristocratic backgrounds. Skill earned Ridge and Rett their positions as Shadows, but men like Finley could not accept that on a field of battle, proficiency made pedigree irrelevant.

Ridge knew Finley resented them for rising above their "place" and then having the audacity to break the rules and succeed more often than anyone else.

"Let's just hope they didn't follow you," Ridge said.

During the long quiet portions of the ride, Ridge had too much time to think about where they were going and what they might find. He and Rett had both come out of past assignments worse for the wear, roughed up by brigands and strongmen, concussed and burned and with broken bones. Torture, thankfully, had been a rarity, and neither of them had endured it for long—candlemarks, not weeks. Not for more than a month.

A very real chance existed that Rett might be damaged beyond even Malachi's ability to repair. Ridge knew that in his head, but his heart refused to accept it. *Rett's strong. Stubborn. He'll fight with everything he's got.*

Until the point where what he had wasn't enough.

If it had been completely up to Ridge, he would have ridden as hard as the horses would allow. Every candlemark they delayed cost Rett blood and pain. But he recognized that Henri was right, much as he didn't want to acknowledge that. Showing up to a fight exhausted with the horses knackered didn't bode well.

Ridge intended for all three of them to survive. That meant pacing their ride, no matter how much he hated losing time. It also required thinking ahead so that they reached Bentham Castle at the right time of day to make their assault. Getting there in broad daylight would mean killing time in a place where they were vulnerable. Better to get in and out quickly and reduce the chance of exposure.

They reached the castle just before sunset. Ridge had the map memorized, but he welcomed the chance to see at least some of the fortification in the fading light. Even without a full garrison, the high stone walls posed a formidable challenge. For Ridge, the hard part wasn't the actual climb; it was making it over the top without being spotted.

Henri might be less exposed going in through the large drain that led down to a creek below the fort, but he faced other dangers since they barely had time to scout the tunnel.

"I'm going to go have a look around," Ridge whispered.

"Keep your head down. I'd rather not have to rescue the both of you," Henri grumbled.

Night reconnaissance was something that felt familiar, part of Ridge's identity as a Shadow, a skill he had honed. Being in "Shadow-mind" made it easy not to think about Rett, not to feel worry or fear. All that mattered was the job, and for the moment, Ridge could shut down all his emotions.

He crept out from the cover of the forest, staying in the darkest areas, sizing up the base of the fortification and the stone walls with the light from the waning moon. Ridge knew from experience that his hook would work in the stone. He watched for movement on the walk along the top of the wall and only saw a single guard make the rounds.

Either Rett's captors felt confident that no one was alive to come to the rescue, or it was a trap. Much as Ridge wanted to believe the first scenario, he had lived this long by considering all the possibilities.

Ridge kept low, using the darkness and the terrain to his advantage. He had the rappelling hook and rope handy and a knife in the other hand.

His instincts warned him even though he heard nothing. Ridge wheeled, knife raised, as a dark form surged up from the ground and tackled him, slamming them both to the dirt while twisting the knife from his grip. A familiar voice made him hesitate.

"It's me, Kane. Ease up."

Ridge saw just enough by moonlight to validate his attacker's statement. "Why—"

"Because it wouldn't be helpful to let you get yourself killed," Kane growled. "I heard about your valet finding someone who could draw him a map." At Ridge's look of surprise, Kane chuckled. "Oh, I hear almost everything."

"Why not just come to us and fill us in?" Ridge wasn't sure whether he'd just been rescued or detained, and anger seemed as good a response as any.

"Because your valet is damn good at disappearing. I followed him partway, then lost him. But I knew where you'd head eventually, and I've been staked out, waiting. That was the only way I figured I'd find you."

"I need to keep moving," Ridge said, pushing Kane off him and sitting up. "Henri's probably already in position."

"He's going in through the runoff corridor while you go over the wall?" Kane asked, then smirked at the expression of annoyance on Ridge's face. "Not a bad plan—but there's a better way out, and there are more guards than I'm betting you banked on."

"How do you know?"

"Whoever's got Rett inside isn't the first to use Bentham Castle since it became inactive. That makes me have all kinds of questions about who's behind this—since there's a very short list of people with the access, or the balls, to use the castle as a secret torture site."

"You've held prisoners there yourself," Ridge said, guessing at Kane's meaning.

"The point is, I've been inside in the past two years. Modifications were made." Kane didn't bother replying to Ridge's question, which was answer enough.

"Shit. Is Henri in trouble?"

"Not yet. I'll lead him around the problem spots. You go over the wall."

"I need to kill the guard on patrol," Ridge countered.

"Already done," Kane said with a smirk. "You're welcome."

Ridge rolled his eyes at Kane's smugness. "Would they hold Rett somewhere other than the jail?"

Kane shook his head. "Doubtful. Given his reputation, they won't leave anything to chance, which means they'll want bars to keep him in. Getting him out is the easy part. We're going to need to kill some people before we get to that point—and you should be asking who took him and why."

"Oh, believe me, I am," Ridge assured him. "And they'll pay. But first... I need to get Rett out of there."

"Come over the wall, and kill anyone you encounter," Kane told him. "If you find civilians, disable them and make sure they aren't going anywhere. They're going to hold the key to what happened at Sommerelle."

"What are you going to do?"

"After I get Henri inside safely and show him the second exit, I'm going to circle the wall and get rid of the guards while you and Henri save your partner," Kane replied.

Ridge looked askance at Kane. "Why are you helping us?"

"I didn't want to see Kristoph dead, and I surely won't like who his killers want as a replacement," Kane replied. "I told you that I'd find you at Sommerelle—before everything went to shit."

"I wondered if you might be tempted to sit this out—at least until the heat was off."

Kane shrugged. "Tempted? Yes. But I gave you my word, and I'm furious about Kristoph. And besides—Malachi sent me."

Ridge knew better than to snicker. He still wasn't exactly sure about the nature of the relationship between Kane and Malachi—and he was smart enough not to ask— but he knew they were very close.

"I saw a man on a fine horse ride in earlier this evening—and didn't see him leave. He'll be the one in charge and perhaps the one behind Kristoph's murder. I doubt he's going to do the messy part himself. Keep an eye out for the torturer as well. As for the rest of the guards, like I said, kill them. By their presence, they have shown themselves to be traitors to the crown," Kane said in a hard tone.

To Kristoph's crown—but what of his successor?

"Unfortunately, I'm nearly out of writs," **Ridge** replied, referencing the legal orders that authorized an assassination in the name of the king. "So if we're caught, we're dead."

Kane shot him a cocky grin. "Then we'd better not get caught."

Ridge slunk silently along the stone wall. When he was in position, he stepped away to swing the iron grappling hook and send it flying, snagging on the top of the wall on the first try. He jerked the rope hard enough to make sure it held and dug the hooks in tight, then started to climb.

This was the easy part; the moves Ridge had practiced and refined over his years as a Shadow. He scaled the wall quickly and noiselessly, leaving the rope in case he or Kane needed an alternate way to escape. Ridge dropped in a crouch and drew his knives. The arrangement of buildings inside the walls matched Henri's drawing, making it simple for Ridge to get his bearings.

They had assumed one guard would watch the main gate and the road, another would patrol along the wall. Kane had taken care of the outside patrol. Ridge felt certain there would be at least one guard near the jail. He glanced up at the rope, knowing it would tip off the guard, but there was no helping it.

Need to get to Rett and get him out of here. Worry about the rest later.

Ridge followed the path he had learned from the map to get from his entry point to the jail. He stayed in the darkest shadows, following the wall widdershins, hoping to spot any guards Kane hadn't yet silenced.

He turned off and headed for the jail, a squat building on the outskirts of the barracks and dependencies inside the fortified walls. Ridge froze when he heard footsteps coming from around the corner, with his knife raised and ready.

The guard made the turn, and his mouth opened to shout an alarm when he spotted Ridge, but Ridge sent a blade flying, and it sank hilt-deep into the soldier's chest, dropping him where he stood.

Ridge checked both ways before he sprinted across the open space toward the jail. He didn't catch sight of Kane, but he noted two pools of fresh blood that suggested the spy had passed that way and probably dragged two dead guards inside one of the buildings.

In the moonlight, the uninhabited fortress had a ghostly feel to it, far too quiet and dark. His time in the army and as a Shadow meant being acquainted with plenty of forts and castles. Under normal conditions, an occupied camp hummed with activity day and night. The air smelled of woodsmoke and food. Candles glowed in some of the windows since chores never ended. Conversations carried on the wind, hoof beats and footsteps echoed, and torches lit the enclosure at night.

Bentham Castle, silent and dark, felt haunted. Ridge was glad not to be able to see restless spirits since he had no doubt that a place like Bentham Castle had plenty of them. Kane's comment about the fortress being used from time to time as a secret facility sent a chill down Ridge's spine.

For an assassin, getting killed in the line of duty went with the job. Few assassins died of old age—and those who appeared to do so vanished to reinvent themselves under a new alias. Ridge had never feared a clean, quick death. But being captured, interrogated, tortured—broken? That froze the marrow of his bones. Knowing that fate had befallen Rett made Ridge remorseless in his need to take out his anger on a worthy target.

Which is why he didn't hesitate when he saw a figure sneaking away from the jail. Ridge knew at a glance that the silhouette didn't belong to Kane—too tall, too thin, and moved all wrong. It didn't strut like a guard or swagger like an aristocrat. That left one likely suspect—the interrogator who had brought Rett to death's doorstep.

Kane and Henri would get Rett's cell open and bundle him for the ride. Although Ridge felt a pang of guilt for not being there first, the need to deal with the man who hurt Rett burned too brightly to ignore.

Whoever the man was, Ridge guessed he didn't have true military training, given the jerky, panicked way he moved. That made it almost too simple for Ridge to come from behind and fling a dagger into the back of the man's right knee.

The stranger fell with a cry of pain, too quiet to raise an alarm. Bleeding, nearly hamstrung, the man tried to get to his feet and failed. He crawled, desperate to evade his pursuer.

Ridge grabbed him by the collar and hauled him up against a wall, with a knife to the throat in case the man had any delusion of fighting his fate.

"Who are you?"

The man in his grasp looked utterly ordinary, not the twisted madman it would be comforting to imagine tortured for pay. Thinning hair, unremarkable features, nothing particularly memorable. Now that his own life was in danger, the inquisitor paled, stammering as he tried to explain himself.

"No one important. Please—let me go."

Ridge slammed him against the wall again, hard. "There's only one reason for someone to be here, and that involves the prisoner who was snatched from Sommerelle when King Kristoph died." He looked the man up and down and saw only a craven functionary. "Start talking, or there's no point to keep you alive."

"No! Don't kill me! I will tell you anything you want to know." The sour smell of urine filled the air as the man pissed himself.

Ridge poked the point of his knife into the man's throat just hard enough to draw blood. "Your prisoner—did you torture him?"

"I—"

"Don't lie to me. I'll know." Ridge slammed him against the wall and kicked his bad knee.

"Yes! Yes. But I didn't strike him. I swear it. The Duke—he likes to hit people."

Ridge didn't have time to take the man's full confession. "You made a big mistake when you roughed up my partner. My *brother*. I should slit your throat and gut you like a hog for slaughter."

The man whimpered.

"You can dish it out, but you can't take it, can you?" Ridge muttered. "I'm going to tie you up and take you with us."

"You're not going to kill me?" The abject hope in the man's voice was laudable—and naive.

Ridge leaned close enough for the man to feel his breath. "Oh, I'm going to kill you for what you did to my partner. The question is—do I do it fast or slow? That's up to you. Be useful, tell me who you work for, give me any details that might be helpful, and I'll make it quick. I'm an assassin. I know how to kill." He shrugged, dragging the point of the knife to make a shallow cut, reinforcing his message, "Or I can pull every answer out of you one sinew at a time. Your choice."

Ridge didn't give the man time to respond. He didn't trust his own impulses. Everything in him wanted to slit the torturer's throat or drive the knife into his heart for what he had done to Rett. But the professional in him, the soldier, knew the mission came first.

Get the information. Then kill the informant.

Without waiting for an answer, he brought the hilt of his knife down hard on the man's head and caught him as he slumped. Ridge tore strips from the man's shirt to tie his wrists and gag him, using his belt to tie his ankles, then grabbed him by the collar and dragged him to the jail.

"Took you long enough," Kane chided as Ridge entered.

"I finished a couple of loose ends," Ridge remarked, dropping the bound and gagged interrogator at Kane's feet.

The spy raised an eyebrow. "Well, well. What an interesting fish you've hooked."

"Where's Rett?" Ridge started to shove past Kane, but the other man grabbed his arm hard enough that Ridge couldn't shake free.

"Henri is with him. Go softly. It's bad." The unlikely compassion in Kane's eyes sparked for just an instant before it hardened, and the spy kicked the bound prisoner in the kneecap as the man started to rouse. He squatted to be nearly on eye level with the torturer.

"This all ends tonight," Kane swore. "You and your sick master, the kidnapping, the torture. You messed with the wrong people. And we're going to make an example of you."

The interrogator whimpered, and Ridge looked at him in disgust. *He didn't mind doing much worse to Rett. I should feel sorry for him— but I don't.*

Ridge noticed the bodies of two guards heaped in the corner. They were missing parts of their uniforms, and Ridge guessed Henri had stripped them to dress Rett for the ride home. "Nice work," he said to Kane.

"I killed two more outside—they were sloppy."

"And I killed one. How many more do you think are here?"

Kane shrugged and did a quick count. "That's six down altogether, including the one I killed outside the walls. As for how many there are—let's not find out."

"Let's get Rett out of here—and this piece of shit," Ridge added, toeing their prisoner in the ribs, "before the other guards wake up."

"Go help Henri. I'll keep watch," Kane told him.

Ridge braced himself, but that still didn't prepare him for what he saw. Rett lay on a filthy cot. Blood covered his ragged clothing, and old, half-healed bruises colored his face and torso. A swollen eye and fresh split lip provided more damning evidence against his captors.

Henri had managed to get a pair of pants and some boots onto Rett—clearly pieces from the stolen uniforms—but wasn't having much luck maneuvering him into a jacket.

"He won't wake up," Henri said, distraught, from where he knelt beside Rett. "I've called his name, shaken him lightly—nothing rouses him."

Maybe that's a mercy, although it'll make the ride that much harder. "Let's finish getting him dressed and get out of here." Ridge helped steady Rett so they could gentle him into the coat.

"Did you or Kane see anything around here that they might have used on him? Can you have a look around?" Ridge went on. "Look for potions, elixir, powders. If we take it with us, maybe we can figure out an antidote."

Henri nodded and got to his feet, then made an efficient circuit of the room. He found a cloth bag and stashed anything in it that looked likely, to examine later. Ridge helped Rett sit up, worried that despite their manhandling, he hadn't woken.

He's got a pulse, and he's breathing. We can work out the details later.

"We've got trouble!" Kane called from the outer room.

"Stay with him," Ridge told Henri as he eased Rett to the floor.

Henri pulled a knife from the sheathe on his belt. "I've got him. We'll be here."

Ridge found Kane to one side of the door, knives drawn.

"They know we're here," Kane murmured. "I caught a glimpse of at least four of them. might be more."

"Suits me just fine." Ridge was glad for a way to channel his rage after seeing what they'd done to Rett. He glanced toward the doorway and then back at Kane. "I have an idea."

The second floor of the jail held an empty storage room and what had probably been the warden's bedroom. It didn't take Ridge long to slip out of the window and climb to the roof, while Kane provided a distraction below.

"I know you're out there," Kane shouted to the darkened street. Ridge heard a muffled grunt and then a frightened whine. "Show yourselves! I don't think your master would like it if I slit his inquisitor's throat."

Ridge pictured the spy using the bound and gagged torturer as a shield, daring the guards to make a move. Buying Ridge time.

He belly crawled across the roof. From this vantage point, he could see three guards in front of the jail and two more blocking the two exit routes. A quick scan of the other rooftops assured Ridge that none of the guards had taken a sniper position with a matchlock, and he didn't see any of them carrying firearms. Just swords.

Ridge smiled.

He threw three knives in quick succession, catching one guard through the throat and the other two in the chest. They were dead before they hit the ground. The remaining guards came running, as well as a third man who must have been around the back of the building. They shouted and pointed, warning each other, but from the ground there was no way they could reach Ridge.

Three guards rushed the door, no doubt intending to over-power Kane. Ridge lit the rag stuffed in the neck of a bottle of whiskey he had found in the front room and tossed the homemade bomb into the gap between the guards and the doorway, cutting them off with a curtain of flame.

While they were momentarily stunned, focusing on the fire, Ridge sent two more knives flying, dropping all but the last guard who was at too bad of an angle for Ridge to hit. When the remaining man collapsed a moment later, Ridge guessed Kane had seen an opening and took it.

Kane might technically be a spy and not an assassin, but he's got skills. Good to know—important to remember.

Ridge waited, sure that if any other guards had been hiding that they would be drawn out by the fire. When nothing moved after a few minutes, he shimmied back inside through the window and came down the stairs at a run.

He glanced toward the doorway. The flames were already falter-ing, but the diversion had served its purpose.

"Nice touch with the fireball," Kane said with a lopsided grin. "Warn me next time, huh?"

Ridge shrugged, hiding a smile. "I improvised." He looked down at the prisoner and then back to Kane. "What about the man in charge? You think he's still here?"

Kane shook his head. "Doubtful. Probably lit out of here at the first sign of trouble. Why wouldn't he? Saved his own ass and left them to take the blame."

"We need to figure out who's behind this," Ridge said.

"We will. I have some connections I haven't tapped," Kane replied. "But first, let's get out of here, in case anyone else comes looking."

Ridge returned to the cell where Henri had Rett sitting upright again.

"Come on, lad. Just a sip," Henri coaxed, holding a battered tin cup to Rett's mouth. Rett parted his swollen, split lips, but he seemed to lose as much water down the front of his shirt as got into his mouth.

"He's running a fever," Henri told Ridge, then frowned and sniffed the air. "Why do you smell like smoke and whiskey?"

Ridge sighed. "Long story. Let's get him on his feet." Ridge squatted to get his shoulder under one of Rett's arms, and Henri did the same on the other side. They half-carried, half-dragged Rett out to the front. When Kane saw them, he hefted the prisoner and put him over his shoulder, leaving one hand free to hold a knife.

"Follow me. I can get us out through the commander's secret exit," Kane told them.

"You think that's how the man in charge got away?" Ridge asked, also armed with a knife just in case they hadn't eliminated all of the guards.

"Maybe—but if so, that raises a lot of questions. I found it by accident because I'm a nosy son of a bitch—probably why I'm a spy," Kane said as he led them through the grounds of the deserted fortress with the confidence of someone who had spent time there. "The exit isn't on any map. I found out that the fortress had a few features that were supposed to be passed down within the family that built it and known to a very few senior officers of the garrison. Which makes me wonder—"

"How did the person who set this up find out?" Ridge finished for him.

"Exactly."

Kane lit a candle from the small pack he carried and led the way inside one of the buildings, to a tunnel hidden behind a false panel in the commander's office. The narrow passage required Ridge to put Rett over his shoulder, and even then he had to angle his body to fit. That meant being extra cautious to keep his footing on the narrow, time-worn rock steps.

Like the passageway Henri and Kane had used to enter, this tunnel also came down to the riverbank, but a ways upstream from the other entrance. Ridge and Henri shifted Rett back to carry him between them, and the trek to where they had hidden their horses seemed to take forever.

The prisoner shifted and fidgeted until Kane finally threatened to drag him by the ankles. Ridge worried about Rett's silence, the fever he could feel even through the stolen jacket, and the fact that Rett bore none of his own weight. He gritted his teeth, stifling the urge to kill their prisoner for the damage done, reminding himself that finding the one who gave the orders was worth the wait.

Kane brought his horse around so they could travel together and slung the prisoner behind his saddle over the horse's rump, fastening him in place with rope. Ridge put Rett across his lap, unwilling to have him out of his sight. Keeping contact meant Ridge could feel reassured that Rett was still breathing.

"Hang on," Ridge told Rett under his breath as they rode as fast as they dared. "Just hang on a little longer until I can get help. Please, Rett. Don't let go."

CHAPTER NINE

*T*hey fled across rooftops, leaping the gaps between buildings, outrunning flames that reached high into the night sky. Rett led the way. Ridge carried the young hostage on his back, the boy they had rescued from an arms smuggler who had taken him as surety for his father's compliance. Only a bit farther, and Henri would meet them with the carriage, whisking them away before the guards arrived.

Rett leaped over the last break between roofs—one that was a little wider than the others.

"Come on," he urged Ridge. "Henri will be coming any minute."

Ridge paused as if assessing the distance with the extra weight he carried. The boy was far too young to make such a leap himself.

"Hurry!"

Ridge backed up a few steps and then took off running. He sprang off the edge, leaning forward, leg outstretched to land. His foot came down, and the edge of the second roof broke under his weight.

Rett heard the sound of splintering wood, the boy's piercing scream and Ridge's loud curse. He ran back, hoping that Ridge had caught a handhold, but he was too late.

The two bodies hit the cobblestones, hard. Blood spattered, bones snapped, and they lay still in a twisted pile.

"No! That isn't what happened. We got out safely. No one fell. Ridge lived. The boy lived. No, no, no!"

The familiar, recurring nightmare shimmered and twisted into a new horrific scene. *Rett recognized the grand dining room at Sommerelle, full of dignitaries. King Kristoph looked solemn and resplendent as he ascended the dais to make farewell remarks before they all raised a goodbye toast and adjourned to mingle.*

Rett edged closer, trying to be inconspicuous and protective at the same time. A servant pushed a cart of cheese and wine close to the edge of the stage for Kristoph to make the toast. Rett's gut urged him to take a few more steps toward the king, putting himself between the monarch and the cart despite the side-eye that Kristoph gave him, warning him against encroaching.

Sudden bright light blinded Rett, and flames engulfed him, burning away his clothing and hair and charring his skin. The ceiling came down, making rescue impossible, leaving the screaming, sobbing victims to roast alive amid the embers...

"I won't use as much this time."

Rett opened his eyes to see Doctor in front of him, holding a jar of noxious paste and a wide blunt knife to spread it over Rett's skin as if he were buttering bread.

Rett tried to pull away, but his bonds kept him in place.

"Struggle... good. Drives blood to the skin," Doctor said, bending to look Rett in the eyes. "Takes the potion to the heart that much faster. You know why witches call it 'flying ointment'? Because it breaks down all barriers. Your will. Your identity. The bond between your body and soul. I'll use less this time... and do more doses. You'll tell us everything we want to know."

Rett struggled until the ropes dug bloody furrows into his wrists and ankles, but the bindings wouldn't break. He twitched and jerked as Doctor smeared a thin skim of foul-smelling paste across the skin on his arms.

"I think... the place where your heart jumps closest as well," Doctor said, after standing back to consider his handiwork. He reached out once again, leaving a smear of ointment on the pulse point in Rett's neck.

Rett felt the effects almost immediately as his stomach swooped, and his breath came in fast, shallow pants. His thoughts slowed, but his pulse raced, and the result was a dizzying swirl that seemed to tilt the world on its axis, as his vision distorted everything he saw into monstrous images.

"Now, tell us where you hid the children," Doctor prompted. "We really want to know."

Rett's screams reached a deafening crescendo, and he felt like his body might turn itself inside-out as reality twisted. The surface of his skin froze and his blood boiled. Air burned like fire in his lungs. He gasped for breath. Rett swore he could feel his eyes bulge and his throat swell shut.

"Where are they?" Doctor urged. "Tell me, and I'll give you the antidote. I can make it stop. Just tell me where they are."

"Go...fuck...yourself," Rett rasped, lisping as his tongue felt too big for his mouth.

Rett's heart pounded, and his head felt like it was being crushed in a vise. Nothing existed except the pain and distortion—not language or even memory. Then everything went black, and Rett fell through darkness, on and on, never reaching the bottom.

He startled awake to find himself in the monastery library. Tom chuckled. "You drifted off for a while. Good dreams?"

Rett tried to slow his breathing as he realized that the pain was gone, as well as the disorientation. He welcomed the respite, except that he once again found himself in a place he didn't remember visiting in person, with a man he was certain he had never really met.

"Yeah. Sure," he replied, because the truth wasn't an option.

"How are you doing on the research?" Tom asked. "Making progress?"

Rett looked at the illustrated manuscript in front of him and the piece of parchment with a quill and ink well off to the right. He saw notes in his own handwriting that he didn't recall inscribing, and the tome was completely unfamiliar.

"I think so," he answered, trying not to give away just how terrified he felt. Everything about the library felt real and solid—the chair beneath him, Tom, the feel of the parchment and the smell of the ink, the faint drift of candle smoke in the air.

Did the "flying ointment" really transport me somewhere else? Or am I still in my head, in another nightmare?

Curious, Rett looked up at Tom. "How are people taking the news? About what happened to the king?"

Tom glanced at him, dismayed and concerned. "What happened to King Renvar?"

Rett's eyes widened. *Renvar? That was King Kristoph's father. Kristoph's been on the throne for fifteen years. Could he really have had no outside news in that long?*

Rett cleared his throat to cover his reaction. "Just that he's been ill of late."

"Ah. I hope he recovers soon. No one has said anything about it—then again, we hear very little from the world beyond the walls," Tom replied. "It's peaceful here like that."

Rett opened his mouth to reply when his vision went white, and a stab of excruciating pain made him grab his temples and slip from his chair to the floor. He heard Tom's worried shout but couldn't manage a reply.

Rett! Things are not as they seem. Hurry—I can hold back the illusions, but only for a moment. Follow Edvard. Go now! Sofen's face came into focus in Rett's mind, dispelling the monastery library. The psychic boy's face faded, and Edvard's ghost stood in the darkness.

"Follow me. Hurry."

The pain vanished with the vision of Sofen. Rett followed Edvard's faintly glowing figure through darkness so thick he couldn't tell anything about his surroundings. His Sight was no help, although he could hear shuffling feet and murmuring voices in the unbroken night.

Where are we going? he asked Edvard, trying to keep up. He hoped the path remained smooth because he couldn't see obstacles or pitfalls.

"Home."

Am I dead? Did you come to lead me across the Veil?

Edvard paused to look over his shoulder. *"Not yet."*

Rett took a long, sudden gasp, and his eyes flew open. He looked around in a panic, and for a moment, nothing made sense.

"Rett? Hey, calm down. You're alright. You're safe. Home." Ridge reached out to grab Rett by the shoulders, but Rett shied away, staring at this new apparition in terror.

"Steady. Steady. Breathe. I'm real. You're actually here. Out. Safe." Ridge just kept repeating the words until their meaning began to sink into Rett's scrambled mind.

"How?" The sound of his own raspy voice made Rett wonder how long he had been screaming.

"We got you out. You're at the cabin. Needed you to wake up and for the poison to wear off." Ridge looked different than before. Worn, haggard—defeated. Dark circles beneath his eyes gave him a hunted, haunted appearance, and the untrimmed beard made Ridge look older.

"Poison?" Everything seemed so real—the feel of the bed linens under his hands, the look of the room, even the smell of firewood and roasting onions. *If this is another illusion, it's the cruelest of all.*

"Yeah, some kind of paste—" Ridge's mouth kept moving, but the room blurred as if reality pulled away from him. Darkness claimed him again, and screams, howls, and shrieking filled the endless blackness.

Rett tried to hold onto that image of Ridge, taking comfort in not being alone in the night, even if Ridge had been just another hallucination. It had been a mercy when all of the other nightmares ended.

Chapter Ten

"**D**ammit! He was back—for a moment, Rett was back!" Ridge stood and kicked the chair out of the way, pacing outside the cabin bedroom as Kane and Henri looked on.

"Are you sure—"

Ridge's death glare silenced even Kane. "Yes. I'm sure. He saw me. He responded with words. And then...he just slipped away again." Ridge barely suppressed the urge to punch the wall, knowing from experience it didn't satisfy.

"I've heard about different ointments like that used in interrogation—if the questioner is someone with magic," Kane said. "Some ointments force a person to tell the full truth. Others eliminate inhibitions. A few can make a person suggestible enough to fill their head with orders and have them carried out without the person ever remembering why."

"Shit," Ridge muttered. "That's bad stuff."

Kane nodded with a grim expression. "Definitely illegal and totally unethical—even in my business. But his reaction makes me wonder—what did they want from him, and was the questioner skilled enough to use the right potion? Because that sort of ointment was also used in rituals to give the participant a 'spiritual experience'—hallucinations."

Henri snorted. "Like the funny mushrooms you can buy in the alley behind the sailor's pub?"

Ridge had heard about those mushrooms and other sorts of plants and mixtures that could put a man out of his head when whiskey didn't suffice to forget the pain of wounds—or life.

"He 'surfaced' like he was coming out of a nightmare," Ridge said, glancing back toward the door to Rett's room. "He'd been flailing and moaning, muttering, but none of it made sense."

Henri nodded. "Aye. We heard him."

"Burning with fever, cold the next moment, twisting like he had a knife in him and then throwing a punch at something only he could see," Ridge went on. It shredded his heart to see Rett suffering, to see his vibrant, resourceful partner turned into a candidate for the madhouse.

"If you'd like to take out your mood on an appropriate target, the inquisitor woke up," Kane said in a dry voice.

Ridge glanced to Henri.

"I'll stay with Rett," Henri promised. "If anything changes, you'll hear me yell."

Ridge and Kane headed out to the barn, where Kane had stashed their prisoner. Kane carried the bag that held all of the items Henri could grab from the jail at the fortress, and Ridge fully intended to find out how to cure Rett or experiment with the substances on the interrogator.

The smell reached Ridge before he saw the crumpled, bound form. "He reeks."

"That goes with fouling yourself," Kane noted, disgust clear in his voice. "Oh, and I think he puked too."

"Lovely."

Ridge hung the lantern from a hook and dragged a bench over, while Kane hoisted the man by his collar and gave him a teeth-rattling shake.

"Wakey-wakey," Kane sing-songed. "We have questions. You've got answers." He sat the man down hard on the bench and ripped the gag out of his mouth. "Starting with your name."

The prisoner licked his dry lips. "Fulton."

Kane held a tin cup of water to the man's mouth, and he drank it all. Kane smiled and crouched to be at eye level. "Alright, Fulton. Who do you work for?"

The man glared at him. "I can't tell you that."

Kane stood and made a show of looking around them. "He's given you up. I don't think he'll be here to save you. You owe him nothing."

Ridge took a step forward with a look on his face few men had survived seeing. "You and whoever you work for plucked Rett from the king's side when the king was murdered. That tells me your master had something to do with the king's death." He bent over to be right in the man's face, close enough to smell the sour odor of fear and the prisoner's rank breath.

"Do you know what they do to king-killers? The gibbet's too good for them. They're flayed, drawn, and quartered, and then burned alive." He let that sink in as the man's eyes went wide and panicked. "Cooperate, and we'll put a knife through your heart. Easy. Quick."

"I've seen men flayed," Kane mused aloud. "Messy. Takes a long time. And they're conscious for the whole thing. I never realized how much skin there was on a human body until I saw it removed, like a glove—"

"The Duke of Letwick," Fulton said. "He dragged me into this—"

"Ridge stood back and let the spy do what he was trained to do—extract information.

"Why did the Duke of Letwick want to kill King Kristoph?" Kane asked.

Fulton whimpered. "I don't know. I really don't. I owed the duke money, and he knew I had been an interrogator in the army. Said he had a job for me that would cancel all my debts. I didn't know he was going to kill the king. I swear I didn't."

Ridge almost felt sorry for the man, who seemed on the verge of pissing himself again. Then he remembered how broken and wounded Rett looked, tossing on his bed, lost in nightmares, and his resolve hardened. "Why did you take Rett?"

Fulton licked his lips again. "It wasn't planned. A last-minute decision. The duke's witch realized he was a Shadow—one of the assassins we were supposed to look for." He glanced nervously at Ridge. "You were the other one."

Ridge laid out the items Henri brought from the fortress. "I want to know what you used on my partner."

The interrogator didn't look so tough now. Bruises mottled his face, and blood crusted at the corner of his mouth. "Some of everything," he muttered.

Ridge drew a deep breath and let it out, trying to keep from killing the man right then and there. "Where did you get the potions? Who's your witch?"

"I don't know—"

Ridge had the point of a wicked knife under the man's chin. "I am one of the King's Shadows. You hurt my partner. My brother. I can make your death quick—or very, very slow. So I want you to think very carefully before your answer. Who is your witch?" He emphasized each word with a poke of the knife.

The man's Adam's apple bobbed as he swallowed hard. "I don't know. Never saw him. The duke brought that stuff with him and said he already knew how to use it. I did what he told me to do."

"Then tell us what you did—and how to fix it," Ridge growled. He withdrew the knife, leaving the underside of Fulton's jaw bleeding where he had been poked. "Is there an antidote?"

Fulton licked his lips nervously, then shook his head. "Not to my knowledge. I told the prisoner we'd give him one if he cooperated, but... I lied."

"Go on," Kane said in a cold voice.

"The duke just wanted to beat the information out of him, but the prisoner wouldn't tell him anything. I've seen that type before. He'd have died before he gave anything up. I told that to the duke," Fulton said, speaking rapidly. "I got him to let me have a go at the prisoner with the potions and ointments."

"Go on," Kane prompted.

"Opium didn't loosen his tongue. I gave him a mix of datura, henbane, and salvia. Laced his food and water with it. That got him to talk, but nothing he said made sense, and he wouldn't answer questions."

Ridge clenched his fist so tightly that his fingernails dug into the palm of his free hand. He had heard about those plants and knew that they were sometimes used when questioning prisoners, particularly if the stakes were high. Without careful oversight, even small doses of those plants could be deadly.

"The duke wanted answers. He didn't want to be at the fortress any longer than necessary. I think he was afraid someone would come after us." Fulton grimaced. "He was right."

"Back to the question," Ridge demanded. "What else did you give Rett?"

"The duke's witch gave him 'flying ointment' to try when nothing else worked. I used too much the first time, and he was too gone to answer anything for days." Fulton licked his lips nervously, warily eyeing Ridge as if he expected a blow.

Ridge restrained himself from dealing out vengeance, but only because he knew that when they had their answers, Fulton would die.

"And then?" Kane asked.

"The next time, I used less, didn't put it on as thick. He dislocated his shoulder trying to get away, but he didn't come out of the trance. Like he couldn't find the way back. Or he didn't want to."

Ridge lunged at the man, knife already in his hand. Kane grabbed him by the shoulders, holding him back.

"Ridge," Kane hissed.

"You saw what he did to Rett—"

"Rett's alive," Kane pointed out, still blocking Ridge's path to the prisoner and restraining him with a painfully tight grip.

"Barely! He's locked inside his head, and we don't know if he'll ever come out."

"All the more reason to find out what we need to know to help him."

"He just said there's no antidote," Ridge argued, pointing at the interrogator.

"That he knows of," Kane bit off each word, meeting Ridge's gaze to convey what he didn't say. *But Malachi might.*

Ridge threw Kane's hands off him with a grunt and turned on his heel, walking off his rage. But he did not try to attack Fulton again, and after a few moments, sheathed his knife.

"What did you want Rett to tell you?" Kane knew how to get information out of an unwilling witness, and he was turning on the empathy, encouraging Fulton to please him with answers since Kane was "protecting" him from Ridge.

He's a spy. I'm an assassin. He gathers information. I kill people who deserve it. And right now, I can't think of anyone who deserves it more than Fulton... except for the duke and his godsdamned witch.

"He wanted to know where the partner was," Fulton replied, with a nod toward Ridge and a wary expression. "And he wanted names of their allies, whether or not they had witches working with them, and whether the rumors were true about the two of them being witchy, also."

"Seems like a big risk to take for little value. What else?" Kane pressed.

Fulton's gaze darted between Kane and Ridge. "He wanted to find out what you knew about Yefim Makary. And about the duke himself. I think... I think he was afraid that you knew he was part of the plot to kill the king and wanted to know who you might have told." He paused. "Mostly, he wanted to know where some children were."

Ridge felt his heart sink. Rett had held out against torture, but if something important slipped out against his will while he was in the grip of the poisons, Lady Sally Anne and her wards might be in danger.

"What did Rett tell you? I want to know everything." Ridge knew he sounded every bit as dangerous as he was. From Fulton's panicked expression, it appeared he understood his peril.

"He called for you," Fulton replied with a nod toward Ridge. "And someone named Henry. At the end, there was Tom."

Ridge and Kane exchanged a puzzled glance. "Tom?" Kane asked.

"He said something about books and a library," Fulton replied, but that didn't jog Ridge's memory of anyone he and Rett knew.

"What else?" Ridge demanded.

"When I pushed him to answer the questions, he said to 'tell Old Muleface to suck eggs.'"

Despite the circumstances, Ridge couldn't resist a chuckle.

Kane gave him an odd look. "I take it that means something to you?"

"Later."

Ridge sobered and focused on Fulton once more. "What else?"

"Nothing, I swear," Fulton said. "He had, um, remarkable resistance."

That's Rett—stubborn to a fault. Thank the gods.

"The duke—have you tortured for him before?" Kane asked.

Fulton looked away. "Yes."

"Who?"

"There was a man...I think he was a merchant. He was supposed to go down to the border and come back with a servant boy. The boy vanished, and there were...problems. The duke was angry."

Ridge remembered the incident well. He and Rett had broken up a smuggling and counterfeiting operation that benefitted the Witch Lord. They'd also stumbled into a slavery ring that kidnapped young children with budding psychic abilities and brokered them off to the Witch Lord's supporters.

"And what did he tell you?" Kane pushed.

"He said that two brigands set the camp on fire, killed some of the smugglers, and took the boy. He had gone into the woods to take a piss and hid until it was over."

Kane shot a look at Ridge. "You might as well have signed your names. You had to burn it down?"

"There were reasons."

Ridge returned his attention to Fulton. The prisoner fidgeted as if he knew his usefulness was nearly at an end. "And the others you tortured? What did they tell you?"

"There was a man—a rough sort. He was supposed to find people with talents that could be useful and collect them for the duke and his allies. He took them, but then someone set them free. The duke wanted to punish his failure—and find out who stopped his plans again."

Fulton swallowed hard. "The others were informants who failed, spies who couldn't find you and your partner, hired killers who didn't succeed at killing the two of you or those blasted heralds. The duke's been after you two for a while. He was furious that his people didn't snatch both of you, but he was going to take it out on the one we did have."

That revelation chilled Ridge to his core. He and Rett had been in greater danger than they ever realized, and Henri too. They had been careful, kept moving, and kept a low profile, but even with all that, luck had been on their side.

Luck, or perhaps ghosts and more of our allies' magic than anyone let on, Ridge thought, his suspicions growing. Along the way, the two of them had been given a selection of charms and amulets. Perhaps those had played a greater role in protecting them than Ridge had dared hope.

"Where is the duke?" Kane jumped. "If he had any inkling that the fortress had been breached, then he's not just going back to his home. Where is he, and where is his witch?"

"I don't know," Fulton replied. "I was just someone he used when he needed information. He didn't trust me, and I never saw him except in the place he chose, at the time he set."

"How did he know where to find you?"

"I'm a guard down on the docks most of the time," Fulton said. "Mustered out of the army for a bad leg that kept me from marching, but wasn't too bad for me to keep thieves out of warehouses. If the duke needed me, he sent someone to get me. When he was done, he had someone take me back. Always in places like the fortress—rundown, abandoned, out of the way."

"And the witch?"

Fulton shook his head, looking panicky. "Never actually met him. The duke didn't tell me his secrets. I just figured the witch had to be somewhere close because the duke would ride off to get something, and it wouldn't be too long before he was back again."

Ridge knew from Kane's expression that they had both come to the same conclusion. Fulton had told them all he knew, and he was now a liability. Just as Ridge figured the time had come, Henri's shouts brought the questioning to a halt.

"Ridge! Get in here, now!"

"Go," Kane said. "I can take care of it—"

"I'll do it," Ridge said. "I owe it to Rett. Just wait."

Kane nodded, and Ridge took off at a run. He bounded across the yard and into the cabin. As soon as he entered, he could hear Rett's cries and Henri's soothing voice.

"Ridge? Where are you? Ridge!" Rett sounded hurt and terrified. Ridge got to the doorway of the bedroom and found Henri struggling to keep Rett down on the bed. The stout valet had sprawled across Rett, anchoring him with his weight. The potions in Rett's blood gave him a madman's strength, and Henri looked likely to be bucked off at any second.

"It's alright, Rett. I'm here. You're safe. You're home." Ridge started up the litany again, knowing it had worked before, fearing that its effects wouldn't last any longer than the last attempt.

"Ridge." Rett's voice went from panicked to sobbing. "I failed. Failed the king, failed Burke, failed you. I'm so, so sorry. My fault. All my fault."

"Shh. Shh. You did real good," Ridge comforted, sitting close to Rett as Henri rolled off to make room. Rett stopped fighting, but tears and heaving breaths replaced rage and the struggle to flee.

"But the king... oh, gods! The king is dead! The sky fell, and we burned." Rett's eyes were wide, pupils blown dark with fear. He started to fight again, and Ridge grabbed his wrists and held them tight.

"You're safe. I'm here, and so's Henri. We'll worry about the rest when you get better." Ridge heard his voice break, but he forced himself to stay strong.

What if the poisons damaged his mind? What if he never wakes up? There has to be a way, has to be someone who can fix this. Ridge's fears rose, but he forced them down, pushing himself into the cold place inside his mind that let him hone his focus on a mission.

"I thought about mixing a sleeping potion with his tea, but with all the stuff that must still be in his blood driving him wild, I didn't want to do more damage," Henri admitted, looking worried and overwhelmed.

"I don't think we have a choice," Ridge said, although he didn't like the idea either. But after everything Rett had been through, the thought of tying him to the bed was even less appealing. "Go fix something; pick the safest mixture you've got. I'll stay with him."

Henri nodded and headed for the kitchen. Rett slumped, no longer trying to fight, and Ridge hoped that on some level he understood he was safe.

Rett's right hook caught Ridge unaware, slamming into his temple and sending him sprawling. Rett moved fast, making a break for the door. Ridge tackled him, sending them both down in a heap. He and Rett sparred often. They knew each other's moves, and under normal circumstances, they were well-matched.

Now, terror and the potions gave Rett a burst of strength, and the poison-induced madness made him unpredictable. It was all Ridge could do to hold on, even as Rett dragged him across the floor.

"Kane! Need your help!" Ridge figured their bound prisoner could stew for a few moments, but he knew he couldn't hold Rett back by himself much longer.

Ridge heard Henri echoing his call for backup, yelling to reach Kane out at the shed. It took several minutes for Kane to arrive, during which Rett kicked, punched, scratched, and bit, nearly wresting free of Ridge's hold. Ridge knew he would be covered with marks and aching from the hits Rett landed, especially since Rett wasn't pulling his punches.

Kane waded in, grabbing Rett's arms from behind, which let Ridge get to his feet. Ridge knew they had no choice except to restrain Rett for his own safety.

"It's going to take all three of us," Kane said, twisting as Rett tried to bite his arm.

"Henri! We need rope and soft cloths—hurry!"

Henri bustled in with a coil of rope and an armful of clean rags. They managed to get Rett to the bed before he suddenly went limp in their grasp.

"He's out cold," Ridge said, hurriedly checking for a pulse and feeling relief as he felt a steady beat beneath his fingertips. "Let's do this before he wakes up again."

Henri wrapped Rett's wrists and ankles with cloth to minimize the damage from the ropes. Ridge and Kane secured the bonds, and Ridge murmured apologies under his breath.

"I'll stay with him," Henri said. "The tea should be ready now. If he wakes again, I'll get some into him."

Ridge ran a hand back through his hair. "We can't keep going like this."

Kane put a hand on Ridge's shoulder. "We need to get him to Malachi."

Worry and guilt shifted into rage. "Where's Malachi been so far? When we needed him? When Rett went missing?"

Kane's gaze darted away, and Ridge felt sure that there was something Kane hadn't told him about Malachi, something important. Not about what he and the mage were to each other; Ridge didn't care. Something else... fundamental. Ridge had always felt he was missing an important piece of information.

What you don't know can make you dead.

"Malachi couldn't get involved directly. But as soon as he knew what happened, he sent ghosts looking for him—and for you. That's how I found you. He just has to do things his own way. It's complicated."

Ridge couldn't stand looking back at Rett, tied to the bed, too pale, eyes shadowed, face gaunt. "Malachi can keep all the secrets he wants. As long as he saves Rett, I don't care."

Kane nodded. "We need to deal with Fulton. Then I'll get word to Malachi—and pull in a couple of other favors."

Ridge gave him a warning look. "Don't forget, we've got a price on our heads. Everyone thinks we're the ones who killed Kristoph. So—"

"These are men I trust with my life," Kane said solemnly. "I understand the stakes."

Ridge and Kane headed back to the shed. His intuition made him hurry, a gut feeling that something was wrong. Ridge hadn't had a choice about calling Kane away from the prisoner, and now he feared that Fulton had found a way to escape.

Kane opened the shed door, and both men froze at the scene in front of them.

Fulton lay on the floor, still bound to his chair. Some of the items Henri had collected back at the castle's jail, the potions Fulton had used on Rett, had been knocked off the table and onto the floor. A broken jar of the "flying ointment" lay next to Fulton, most of the paste gone, and the blood on the shards made it clear Fulton had licked the contents clean.

His body vibrated, straining at the bonds, head thrown back and mouth stretched in a rictus grin.

"He's having a fit," Kane said as he and Ridge turned the chair so the man lay on his back.

"He ate the ointment." Ridge looked from the bloody, shattered glass to the flecks of paste that remained on Fulton's lips.

"He had to have knocked the jar off the table. Which means it wasn't an accident."

Fulton panted for breath. Heat radiated from his flushed skin, and his eyes were wide and unseeing. Every muscle was drawn tight like a cord stretched to its limit. Fulton had told them that there was no antidote. *What's the point? He didn't know anything else useful. We came back to kill him.*

"I guess he figured that he'd either die by his own hand or be out of his head with the poison when we killed him," Kane said.

"Gods," Ridge muttered. Despite what he'd threatened—and what Fulton deserved for hurting Rett—Ridge had already made up his mind to make the interrogator's death quick. Not for Fulton's sake, but because Ridge had no desire to become the thing he hated.

Ridge drew his knife. "Might as well finish this." He took a step toward Fulton as the man's body jerked, his breath caught, and then he went still.

Kane bent to check for a pulse, alert for a trick and careful not to touch anything tainted by the ointment. After a few moments, he looked up and shook his head. "Dead."

Ridge frowned, still gripping his knife. "How?"

Kane stood, looking down at the corpse. "Put too much strain on his heart, I'd guess. He took a massive dose."

That could have happened to Rett. Did Fulton know how much ointment it would take to kill him? Had he killed other men like that to please his master?

"Guess we need to bury him," Ridge said, pushing the other thoughts away. "I'll start digging."

Kane nodded. "I'll clean up in here. Figure we should save what we can of the poisons for Malachi to look at, see if he can come up with an antidote."

Ridge took a shovel and headed out behind the shed. Digging gave him a way to work off his fear and frustration, translating emotions into physical labor. He focused on the rasp of the shovel, the burn in his shoulders and arms, the smell of fresh dirt.

He thought about just digging a shallow grave, but he liked the cabin. Even if they had to leave to find Malachi, Ridge wanted it to be possible for them to return. That meant it was best not to leave dead bodies lying around. Better to bury him deep.

Kane came out with a second shovel and helped finish the last few feet of the grave. They heaved Fulton's body in, chair and all, careful not to touch any place he had smeared with ointment. By the time they filled in the hole, both men were sweating and breathing hard.

"I wonder how much gravediggers get paid?" Kane mused, leaning on his shovel.

"Not enough," Ridge replied. They returned the shovels to the shed and filled a bucket of water from the well to wash up. The cold water cleared Ridge's head and sluiced away the sweat and grime. Now that Fulton had been dealt with, Ridge's worries returned to Rett and how to find the current Duke of Letwick and bring him to justice.

"I meant to ask you ... who is 'Old Muleface'?" Kane asked.

Ridge chuckled. "Back in the orphanage, when we were little, one of the monks had a very sour disposition, and he was known for never changing his mind—being mulish. Behind his back, everyone called him 'Old Muleface.' That's how I knew it was really Rett talking—at least at that moment."

Henri was in the kitchen, cleaning up. "Rett's sleeping. How did things go?"

"Fulton's dead. He managed to poison himself with the same ointment he used on Rett," Ridge said. "Spared me the effort of slitting his throat."

Henri's mouth was a hard line. "Serves him right."

"I sent a message to a contact of mine, wanting to know more about potions and antidotes. He'll reply—but I can't guarantee how quickly," Kane said as they walked back to the cabin.

Ridge looked at him. "How did you do that? We're in the middle of nowhere, and the carrier pigeons are useless without Burke to receive them—since the Shadows who are left to get the message wouldn't be inclined to help us."

Kane shook his head and smiled. "Ghosts. Malachi sent a spirit to check on us and make sure I was alright. He was worried. This would not be a good time for him to be out and about," he added as if he anticipated Ridge's unspoken question. "I gave the ghost my message, and then Malachi sent a ghost to a mutual acquaintance with my question. I trust Gil to get back to me."

"Gil, who?" Ridge asked, suspicious.

"Gillis Arends," Kane replied, pausing as if he were waiting for them to react.

"Arends? Isn't that the family name for the Earl of Marshbridge?" Henri asked, raising an eyebrow. "Rather chummy with the better sort, aren't you?"

Kane smiled. "Actually, Gil has a lot in common with Ridge and Rett. Turns out he sees and hears and knows things he can't explain," he added with a pointed look at Ridge. "Talks to spirits and gets flashes of things that haven't happened yet."

"And they haven't hauled him off to the army or the priests?" Henri looked intrigued and wary.

"The benefit of having an earl for a daddy," Kane replied with a shrug. "Gil didn't go telling people what he could do—he just went to gambling houses and the secret wagering parties held by the rich wastrel sons of the aristocrats and cleaned them out. Repeatedly."

"Wasn't he rich already?" Ridge couldn't help feeling a grudging admiration for Gil, imagining his fellow gamblers getting their comeuppance.

Kane made a dismissive gesture. "Oh, he didn't need the money. He liked taking them down a peg. Then he started meddling in situations where those outside certain circles would have never heard of the wrongs done—by people who felt certain they were untouchable."

Ridge and Henri exchanged a glance. "Sounds promising," Ridge said.

"The beauty was, he didn't need to involve the guards. Gossip among the aristocrats is deadly business … a word whispered in the right ear, a hint given to the right person." Kane offered a malicious smile.

"I get the feeling there's a 'but' coming," Henri observed.

"Gil got a little too good at dealing out rough justice—and winning at card games. Word reached Kristoph that he might have unpopular abilities. But Kristoph didn't want to alienate Gil's father. So for penance, Kristoph forced Gil to team up with a sheriff who had also drawn his ire for being a little over-zealous, and they were told to work together on cases Burke assigned them—or else."

"Funny that Burke never mentioned them," Ridge said in a dry voice.

"Remember—Gil's penance helped him avoid everyone finding out he has magic," Kane said. "That goes against telling everyone.

Which brings us back to now. I asked Gil to find out who might have been using Bentham Castle and why."

"You don't think it's the Duke of Letwick, like Fulton said?" Ridge asked.

"I don't think he's the only one involved, do you?"

Ridge shook his head. "No. I'm sure there are others. But we still haven't figured out what the connection is between Yefim Makary and the plot for the crown. There's something personal. I'm sure of it."

"Does it matter?" Kane raised an eyebrow.

Ridge thought for a moment, then nodded. "In this case, I think it does. I think there's a reason for the obsession, and if we figure it out, we'll find more of his co-conspirators."

"Gil will know. Those are the kinds of secrets he's very good at ferreting out."

"What makes you think we can trust him?" Henri asked.

"I'm good at finding out secrets too," Kane added with a wolfish smile.

CHAPTER ELEVEN

Just before dawn a knock at the door sent Ridge to his feet, knife already in hand. Kane stirred from where he slept in a chair, similarly armed. Ridge took a careful look out the window and saw a man he didn't recognize. The stranger lowered the hood of his cloak, revealing a handsome, red-haired man. A short distance behind him stood an older, gruff-looking man with dark hair.

Ridge didn't know them and wasn't expecting company.

"Stand down," Kane said. "It's Gil and Luc."

Ridge wheeled on him. "How in the name of the gods did they know where to find us?"

Kane's smug expression nearly moved Ridge to take a swing at him. "Remember those 'special abilities' I mentioned? Gil's a powerful medium—among other things. Might be a good idea to let him in."

Kane went to answer the door. Ridge hung back, sheathing his knife but keeping his hand close to the grip until he felt certain that their visitors meant no harm.

"Gil, this is—" Kane began as he ushered the man inside. Luc stayed outside, presumably on watch.

"Joel Breckenridge," Gil interrupted, identifying Ridge without needing to be told and extending his hand. "One of only two people to give Burke more heartburn than Luc and me."

Ridge shook his hand, finding the grip strong even if the palm was smooth and uncalloused. An aristocrat's hand, not someone who considered digging a grave all in a night's work. "Anyone who gives Burke heartburn is alright in my book."

147

"Burke's alive," Gil said, meeting Ridge's gaze. "I sent the ghosts looking for him as soon as I heard what happened. Looks like he had his own escape plan."

Ridge accepted the news for the peace offering it was. "Thank you. How did you find us?"

Kane drew them into the kitchen, where a pot of coffee warmed in the banked embers. Ridge motioned toward the table, and Kane brought over three cups of the dark, strong liquid.

"Make it four," Gil instructed. "Luc will want some coffee once he comes in from patrolling."

Kane grinned. "I figured if we got one of you, we'd get the other."

Gil shrugged. "My king-appointed ball and chain," he said with an exaggerated sigh.

Ridge had the feeling that there was a lot more in that comment than was spoken, an inside joke he wasn't yet privy to.

"As for finding you, Lorella sent a ghost to ask me to keep an eye out for you, at Lady Sally Anne's behest," Gil finally answered Ridge's question. "Oh, yes. Lady Sally Anne and I know each other. Moved in the same circles until that overblown beast of a husband of hers died. We've kept in touch."

"She and Lorella are pretty amazing," Ridge replied.

"Very true. But I could have found you without their help. For one thing, Rett's pet ghost, Edvard, isn't hard to spot once you know what you're looking for. And you've got one of the herald's medallions on you," Gil continued, eyeing Ridge speculatively. "Interesting plan, by the way. In case you wondered, it did save a number of lives, and when it didn't, the incidents were witnessed, and the information passed on. It helped catch the killers."

"Good to know."

"But these past few days? Your partner's power glows in the Veil like a beacon. It's a damn good thing you've got this place warded because otherwise every ghost and undead thing would have come out of the woodwork—as well as people whose attention you really don't want."

Ridge's heart sank. "Shit. How do we stop that?"

Gil and Kane exchanged a glance. "Malachi," they said in unison.

"I'm good with ghosts," Gil said, "but I'm not a necromancer like Malachi."

"Rett isn't dead," Ridge argued.

Gill shook his head. "No. But the poison that was used on him reacted the way it did because of his abilities. Part of being able to see ghosts that aren't otherwise visible lies in having a touch of magic that pulls back the curtain between the living world and the Veil. The poison thinned that barrier for Rett, which is how his spirit was able to travel to Harrowmont and elsewhere."

"I still don't understand how he could be a ghost if he didn't die," Ridge argued, not wanting to think about the possibilities too closely.

"Not a ghost," Gil clarified. "More of a spirit-traveler. There's a long history of people with abilities being able to go wandering without their bodies under certain circumstances and then return without injury. Especially if they were near death and then revived."

"That's a new ability," Ridge said, feeling a little dizzy at the idea. "I'm pretty sure he would have mentioned something like that if it had happened before."

"One of the reasons practitioners used some of those potions was because of the effect when coupled with magic," Gil said. "Used intentionally, with careful supervision, they could avoid the dangers—most of the time. But from the message Kane sent, that wasn't the case for Rett. So it's not a surprise it blew his doors wide open. It's a wonder he's still alive."

Ridge clenched his fist at the surge of anger that flowed through him, even knowing Fulton was dead. Letwick and his witch were still on the loose, and he felt certain the duke did not act alone.

"What about Letwick?" Kane took a sip of his coffee, curling his lip at the bitter taste.

Gil sat back and crossed his arms. "Did you know that four hundred years ago there were two contenders for the crown of Landria?

Landria hadn't been formed into a proper kingdom yet, just a bunch of warlords consolidating their territories. Of course, the territories around them were also centralizing, so choosing a king to bring the different factions together made sense for protection."

He finished his coffee and set the cup back on the table. "The two strongest contenders were Nolan of Braeden and Rupert of Letwick. Not surprisingly, the two men hated each other. They were both good commanders, but Nolan was more respected, seen as more trustworthy. Then he won a decisive battle, and the other landholders and warlords threw in their lot with him, and Rupert lost his chance at the crown."

Ridge stared at him. "You can't be serious. The Witch Lord killed Kristoph over a four-hundred-year-old grudge?"

Gil shrugged. "Kingdoms have been lost over less. The Letwick fortunes dwindled—probably in no small part because the crown saw the danger of letting them prosper. They were pushed out of roles of any importance at court and fell back to their lands and their vineyards. Those who wanted favor at court avoided the Letwicks, who were effectively ostracized."

"They're still rich," Ridge pointed out. "Still titled aristocracy with lands and manors. So they weren't ruined."

"I guess that depends on the perspective," Gil replied. "Maybe the Letwicks thought they could have done a lot better. The hate and grievances have been festering for centuries. Over the years, every time there was trouble, a Letwick had his finger in it. Too slippery to hang for it, but always on the edges."

"And Makary?"

"Born Thaddeus Letwick Bartleman, from a minor branch of the family—up near Sholl," Gil explained. "Not even a direct descendent of Rupert's. Thought about going into the priesthood, but his father had been rabid on the old legends about the crown, and Thaddeus was ambitious. Then he found a willing accomplice in the current duke, Weston."

Ridge let out a long breath, guessing the rest. "Thaddeus changed his name to Yefim Makary because he knew 'Letwick' would be a red flag, and the other nobles would never go along with a Letwick scheme. I'm sure his followers didn't get the idea of calling him the 'Witch Lord' all on their own."

"Highly doubtful," Kane said.

Ridge thought about the two attempts on Kristoph's life he and Rett had foiled and the one they didn't. "Every attempt has involved events where the other nobles were present. So there must have been more of Makary's supporters than we suspected."

"Knock off the king, and everyone has a chance to move up," Kane observed. "None more so than Weston Letwick. And if you recall, all those schemes resulted in the deaths or imprisonment of a number of nobles. All Weston had to do was sit back, keep his nose clean—at least to appearances—and let Makary recruit the other disloyal nobles, who took the fall when things went wrong."

"And reduced the competition for the real prize—when they succeeded in killing Kristoph," Ridge added bitterly. "We already figured Makary himself didn't want the crown, but he intended to be the power behind the throne. Weston would be indebted to him, and Makary would have enough blackmail to keep Weston under his thumb."

"I don't know if Makary and Weston were really that brilliant or if events just worked in their favor. But yeah, that's what I've been able to pull together from a variety of sources," Gil told them.

Ridge leaned forward. "Where's Weston now? Because I have one last writ of assassination left from the king, and I intend to use it when I kill the son of a bitch—after we take care of Rett."

"Still working on that," Gil admitted. "Clearly Letwick didn't go home after what happened at Bentham Castle. Which—by the way—also belonged to a Letwick relative at one time."

Ridge gave Gil a measured look. "If you could find all of this out so quickly—why wait until now? We've been fighting the Witch Lord for a while."

"We didn't have the Letwick connection to trace back from," Gil replied. "Starting from the other end—who among the disaffected nobility might want to kill the king—was too big of a field of contenders, even for a decent king like Kristoph. Believe me, if we could have prevented what happened, we would have."

"Do you know who Letwick's witch is? I doubt it's Makary him-self—he wouldn't want to get his hands dirty. Because I've got a score to settle with him too." Although magic was technically illegal except for the priests and army, Ridge knew that many noble houses quietly retained a witch who often passed as a "healer."

Gil shook his head. "Not yet. All in good time."

Ridge looked away. He couldn't help considering Kristoph's death to be a personal failure, although he would never have blamed Rett or any of the other Shadows for not preventing it. And now that he'd heard Gil's side of things, he realized that they'd all done their best, and it just wasn't enough.

The temperature in the room plummeted, cold enough that Ridge could see his breath like on a winter morning. The air wavered, then slowly Edvard's ghost took shape, and Ridge wondered if Gil lent him energy to make himself seen.

"You're in danger. Eight well-armed fighters are heading this way."

"Guards?" Ridge asked sharply, already running through their options and weapons.

"No. But dressed in dark colors, with a lot of weapons."

"Shadows," Ridge spat. "I wondered how long it would take without Burke in charge for them to turn on us."

Gil turned to Kane. "Get them out of here. Luc and I will stall the Shadows and meet you later."

Ridge looked at Gil. "There are gunpowder charges daisy-chained with fuses in the shed—set them off, and you'll have a nice distraction. Just don't hurt the livestock. A friend will come for the animals."

Gil gave a sharp nod. He handed Ridge a bag from his belt. "I know you already have some diversion charms. These spell bags will reinforce them. Put them in Rett's pockets—we need to dim his light, so we aren't besieged by every ghost along the route."

Ridge headed for the bedroom, where he could hear Henri gathering what they would need to care for Rett. They had figured it would only be a matter of time before they needed to leave, so their bags were already packed.

Ridge had hoped that they could give Rett as much time to recover as possible before moving him. It would have been nice for the cabin to go unnoticed so they could return, but now that it was compromised, coming back wasn't going to happen. They would take all the supplies and weapons they could carry and leave the rest. He wrote a hurried note for his neighbor Preston and gave it to Kane to pin up in the chicken coop, instructing his friend to take the animals and garden produce.

They'd kept the horses with them this time, in case they needed a quick getaway, and Henri had retrieved their third horse sometime overnight. Kane headed to the barn to ready their mounts, while Ridge went to help Henri.

"What do we do if he has a fit while we're on the road?" Henri asked, already untying Rett and helping him into traveling clothes.

"We'll take it as it comes," Ridge replied. "I'm not going to make him travel in chains like a prisoner." He tucked the spell bags into the pockets of Rett's coat, pants, and shirt.

"Might not hurt, though, to tie him to the saddle," Henri mused. "We don't need him running off."

Rett sat where Henri had put him, looking like a sleepy drunk. Ridge squatted in front of him and made eye contact. "Hey, Rett. You know who I am?"

Rett nodded. His eyes still had a glazed, unfocused look, but his color had improved, and his lips no longer held a bluish tint. Rett was still too thin, malnourished from his captivity, but that would require time to fix.

At least one piece of this is easy to put right.

"We have to go. It's too dangerous to stay. Can you walk?" Ridge asked the question and then held his breath until Rett nodded.

"That's good. Come on then. We need to ride."

"I filled a wineskin with the tea I made for him," Henri said quietly as Ridge pulled Rett to his feet and slung an arm around his waist to support him as they walked as quickly as they dared toward the back door.

Kane had the horses ready, and as Kane and Henri fastened their bags and bedrolls behind the saddles, Ridge helped Rett into the saddle and then looked at him apologetically.

"I don't want you to fall off," Ridge said, meeting Rett's eyes and hoping he was enough himself to understand. "You're not a prisoner. We're trying to get you somewhere safe."

For a moment, he saw a familiar presence behind Rett's brown eyes. "Do it."

Ridge secured Rett and then swung up on his horse. Henri handed up the reins, and Ridge took them, hoping they could get far enough ahead of their pursuers to avoid an all-out chase.

Kane led the way, and Henri took up the rear. Even with weapons handy, Ridge couldn't help worrying about the road ahead—and what would await them when they arrived. The air grew suddenly colder, and Ridge wondered if Gil had sent ghosts to deter anyone who might try to follow.

When they made it to the old timber road Henri had scouted as a possible escape route, Ridge let out the breath he had been holding. The long-unused road was now more of a clearing through the forest, still passable but high with weeds. It angled through the woods, eventually bringing them out to a route north while avoiding more traveled highways closer to where people might be looking for them.

Ridge froze when he heard hoof beats coming from behind them and figured that a couple of their pursuers must have managed to get past Gil and Luc.

"Kane and Henri—take Rett and go on ahead. I'll hold them off."

"You're not expendable," Henri warned, accepting the reins to Rett's horse.

"I can't fight them if I'm worried about protecting Rett," Ridge said. "Go on. Hurry. I'll catch up."

Henri didn't look happy about separating, but he and Kane did as Ridge asked, disappearing over the next rise while Ridge readied his weapons. He led his horse into the woods and tethered him, then slunk back to the edge of the forest and found a perch in an elm on the shoulder of the road. Ridge pulled his crossbow, nocked a bolt, and waited.

Moments later, two dark-clad riders rode into view. Ridge recognized them as Shadows, although not ones he or Rett knew beyond a nodding acquaintance. *Not Caralin,* he thought with relief, more convinced than ever that their ally had probably already gone to ground.

He fired once, taking the lead rider through the chest. The second bolt pierced the neck of the second rider. They wavered for a moment in their saddles as if not sure they were dead, then toppled.

Ridge waited, fearing that more would come this way, hoping that Gil and Luc managed to distract the others. When he heard no other sound of pursuit, Ridge dropped to the ground and led his horse back to the road, riding as hard as he dared to put the bloodied bodies behind him.

Only then did the full impact of what he had done hit him, as the battle coldness of self-preservation waned.

He had killed fellow Shadows in cold blood. Never mind that the charges against him—and Rett—were a lie. The Council of Nobles and whoever took over in Burke's absence would see it as stark betrayal, proof of treason.

In saving their lives, he'd also sealed their fate. There was no going back now.

The cabin was miles behind them when an explosion sent the birds flying in a panic. Ridge glanced over his shoulder and saw a plume of fire and smoke. Gil had either set off the blast to warn off their pursuers or had taken some of them out in the explosion.

We always knew that most of the Shadows disliked us. I guess now we know how much.

Ridge scanned the forest continually for more threats. *Should I feel flattered they thought it might take eight Shadows to capture us?* He couldn't help a pang of disappointment to have his worst suspicions confirmed. Other than Burke, Caralin was the only one of the Shadows who had consistently supported him and Rett, taking risks to help them more than once. Ridge wondered what had become of her.

Does she believe we killed the king, or did she run like Burke? She's good—which means they won't find her unless she wants to be found.

Then again, they managed to find us, and I thought we'd covered our tracks. Of course, Gil and Lorella aren't the only mediums out there. Someone the priests or the army conscripted might have picked up on the ghosts, or someone with talent who supports the Witch Lord. If Rett's abilities are a beacon, there's nowhere we can go that's truly safe.

They rode as hard as they dared, stopping only to give the horses a rest. Kane led the way since he was the only one who knew how to find Malachi. Ridge cast worried glances at Rett as the day grew long, but whatever Henri had put in the tea sedated Rett enough to apparently keep the hallucinations at bay. A few times Ridge thought he caught his partner dozing. They had long ago perfected catching a quick nap in the saddle after hard fights or on long rides, but Rett still had to be heavily drugged to be able to sleep while they were running for their lives.

What if Malachi can't put things right? What if the damage from the poison is permanent?

Shadows didn't die of old age. Most died bloody, defending king and kingdom, going down in the thick of the fight. Those lucky enough not to die in action left because they were too battered to do the job, limping through a few more years before the end.

Now and again, he and Rett had talked about how they saw the future. Those conversations usually came in the dead of night on a long ride or well into a bottle of whiskey celebrating the end of another mission where they weren't dead.

The most hopeful future either of them could envision was mustering out of the Shadows alive but damaged. Despite both of them still being in their twenties, it only took one bad fall or a hard hit to the head to leave someone too broken for the fight. If that ever happened, they had promised each other they would stick together. Ridge just hadn't expected the end to come so quickly.

It's hardly like I'm giving up anything. My days as a Shadow are over. There's a price on both our heads. Probably on Henri and Kane now too.

If Rett never gets better... I'll deal with it. I proved at the cabin that I could raise food to get us by. If I need to, I could probably find work as a farmhand. Bring in some money, stay out of the way. We'll manage. I just thought we'd have a few more years the way it was, but nothing's ever guaranteed—especially not for an assassin.

We had a good run. And the three of us are free and together. That's probably more than I've got a right to ask for.

Kane remained tight-lipped about where they were going, refusing to give specifics other than to say he was taking them to Malachi. Ridge didn't feel like fighting about it since they didn't have any other options.

They stopped when it grew too dark to ride safely and made a cold camp just inside the tree line, far enough into the woods to keep from being visible to anyone on the road. Not that they had passed more than a handful of travelers, all of whom looked like farmers.

Ridge had a decent sense of direction, and he knew from the sky and stars that they were headed farther north. The farms grew fewer, and the woods stretched larger. They were about as far from Caralocia and the power centers of the kingdom as they could get. If they continued to the far reaches, there was little except lumbering, ore mines, and the hard-scrabble farms of those who chose to make their home in these forbidding hills.

To a city boy like Ridge, the territory seemed foreign. Candlemarks passed between settlements. He had spent his life hiding among the crowds in cities, invisible in the press of people. Out here, with no one else around, he felt vulnerable.

Just before sunset, a tall stone tower came into view. Unlike the keep of a castle, no walls surrounded the structure. More to Ridge's concern, he could see no door.

"Where are we?" he asked Kane, who had brought them to a halt some distance away.

"Runed Keep."

Ridge's eyebrows rose, and he could see the look of surprise on Henri's face. "I thought we were going to Malachi."

"Who did you think Malachi was?" Kane asked, with an amused expression.

"Not the most infamous witch in the kingdom!" Ridge felt a combination of anger, fear, hope, and worry. He had trusted Kane to get them to safety. More than that, he had trusted him to get Rett to someone capable of healing him. If Kane had somehow betrayed them—

"There's a long story, and I'll tell it when we're inside," Kane said, and something in his eyes suggested that he guessed Ridge's concerns. "First, I want to make sure there aren't any physical guards. Then, we'll get Malachi to let us in."

"A prison that permits visitors?" Henri sounded curious, but Ridge noted that he had his knife close in case their faith had been misplaced.

"Malachi figured out how to defeat the wardings a long time ago," Kane said. "But he knew if he ran away, they'd just chase him and lock him up again. He decided to stay and let them think he was a prisoner. He comes and goes as he pleases. But this is one reason why we keep his contact with other people at a minimum."

Ridge had plenty of questions, but he knew they needed to get inside. The night had grown cold, and Rett looked utterly spent, drooping in his saddle.

"What now?" Ridge asked, wary about being out in the open, where an archer or marksman could take a shot, and they'd never see it coming.

Kane pulled a necklace with a charm on it from beneath his shirt and let it dangle. "I'm going to ride close and see if there's anyone around. Usually there isn't—but after what happened to Kristoph, they might have decided to send guards. I'll wave you in if it's safe."

He rode off without waiting for an answer. Ridge swore under his breath.

"I didn't expect this little surprise," Henri said, watching Kane's figure recede.

"Me neither. Although I guess in hindsight, it shouldn't have been. Then again, all the stories I've ever heard make the 'mage of Rune Keep' out to be some sort of monster," Ridge replied.

"That's a good way for the king to make sure no one argues to let him go," Henri replied. "Blacken his reputation so badly no one will champion freeing him."

Ridge nodded. "Staying here when he's able to leave is clever of Malachi. It doesn't seem to have kept him from doing what he wants. I get the feeling he sees a lot of Kane."

"There are days when the idea of being at the top of a tower where no one could interrupt sounds pretty good," Henri admitted.

In the distance, Kane waved an "all clear" signal. Ridge, Rett, and Henri rode to join him. Up close, the tower seemed to stretch to the clouds. Huge blocks of stone formed the base, with archer slits staggered around the shaft, presumably to allow light for the stairs Ridge guessed to be inside.

"What about the horses?" Ridge looked around. If guards returned, finding four horses would be a sure giveaway.

"There's a farm about a half a candlemark from here where I board Malachi's horse and mine when I visit. I'll take our mounts as soon as we get Rett situated, and I'll walk back," Kane said.

Ridge and Henri helped Rett down from his horse. He looked exhausted from the ride, but the weariness in his eyes and the gauntness of his face suggested a much deeper strain. They shouldered their bags, and Ridge cast a doubtful look up the length of the tower, anticipating a long climb.

"Light a lantern," Kane instructed. "The stairs aren't bad in day-light, but you won't see a thing now that it's night."

"How do we get in?" Henri asked.

Kane closed his hand around the amulet and shut his eyes, con-centrating. A moment later, the wall of the tower wavered, and a door appeared in what had been solid stone.

"Go ahead," Kane urged. "I'll catch up. Malachi's been expect-ing us."

Ridge reached for the handle of the thick iron-bound oaken door, and he wouldn't have been surprised if his hand went right through. To his relief, cold iron met his grip, and the door yielded when he pulled. Henri took a candle and lantern from their bags and lit it, holding it aloft.

"Leave any bags you can't carry at the bottom," Kane said. "I'll bring them with me. After the first visit, I started leaving some of my things here rather than carry them up or down. The guards never go to the living quarters."

They got Rett inside, and Kane shut the door behind them. When Ridge looked back, the wall was solid once again.

Henri lifted the lantern, illuminating the curling stone stair-case that stretched out of sight in the darkness. "I guess we'd better get climbing."

"You still with us, Rett?" Ridge asked worriedly. Rett looked dazed, but he managed to keep his feet under him, and once they began to climb, the set of his jaw proved Rett would give the effort his best.

The stairs were too narrow to walk three abreast. Henri went first with the lantern, then Ridge slung Rett's arm over his shoulder and sidled up, one step at a time.

"Welcome," Malachi said, standing framed in the doorway at the top. He held a lantern out over the steps to light their way. "Come in. I've been waiting for you."

Ridge hadn't known what to expect of Malachi's prison. He had imagined a round, stone-walled dungeon room, bare of anything but meager necessities. Instead, he found three floors comfortably outfitted to accommodate a mage of presumably noble birth. *Not too bad for an exile, considering the alternatives.*

"Bring him into the kitchen." Malachi led the way. "Eat and drink first. Then we'll see what I can do to help." As he spoke, his gaze played over Rett, sharp and assessing despite the casual tone of his welcome.

"Supplies are delivered once a week—food, parchment, firewood, ink, whiskey, and the like. It's part of the spell put in place when the king exiled me. The supplies are delivered to a particular spot. Nothing living can be in the bundles. The spell transports them inside to the entry area, where I have to retrieve them. It's a one-way spell, in case you wondered," Malachi told them. "There's a cistern on the ground floor for water."

"And you've been here how long?" Ridge asked, helping Rett get seated at the table.

"Ten years," Malachi replied. "As you may have guessed, I've made a few…modifications…over the years." He winked. He and Kane were older than Ridge and Rett. Malachi appeared to be late in his third decade, with long dark hair, high cheekbones, and vivid green eyes.

A simple soup plus bread served as dinner—easy to cook and useful to stretch ingredients, Ridge figured, since Malachi wasn't supposed to have company. Despite their long ride and a supper of trail rations the night before, Rett needed to be coaxed to eat. He moved like a sleepwalker, able to follow simple directions but otherwise sitting and staring. The difference between Rett now, drugged and pliant, and his usual vibrant curiosity and quick wit broke Ridge's heart.

As they ate, Ridge and Henri took turns catching Malachi up on what had happened since they had last seen him and about Rett's kidnapping and torture.

"So the duke who was behind taking Rett also schemed to kill the king?" Malachi asked, anger clear in his voice.

"Yes. And according to Gil and Luc, there's even more behind it." Ridge filled in the latest information from their recent visitors.

"You three have really landed in it, haven't you?" Malachi said, shaking his head. "Alright—first, I need to have a good look at Rett. Do you know what he was dosed with?"

Henri dug the small bag of poisons out of his pack and passed it to Malachi. "Minus most of the flying ointment, which the torturer ate," Ridge said.

"I suspect that ended unpleasantly."

Ridge drummed his fingers on his thigh beneath the table, trying to be patient as Malachi examined the poisons, and then took a close look at Rett. Henri explained the ingredients of the sedative tea, and Malachi nodded, taking it all in.

"Can you help him?" Ridge finally burst out. "It's like he's locked in his own head, and I don't know how to reach him."

Malachi pushed his chair back and laid a reassuring hand on Rett's shoulder. "You're right," he said to Ridge. "That's exactly what happened. Part of it is battle fatigue from the torture. When there's no escape possible and no rescue likely, the mind turns in on itself to survive. I don't doubt that they told him you and Henri were dead."

Malachi's voice remained calm, but Ridge saw a new tension in the man's body and took it for anger at Rett's mistreatment. "I recognize the potions that were used on him. Nasty stuff. Doesn't take much to be deadly. They would cause symptoms that made him feel like he was dying. That alone put a real strain on his system. But the ointment—" He shook his head, and Ridge's heart sank.

"Is there nothing you can do?" he asked, sounding broken and lost, even to himself.

Malachi met his gaze. "I'm not giving up, not yet. There may be an antidote—and if not, I can create elixirs to counter some of the effects and use magic to offset others. But even with all that, it may not be enough."

Ridge looked down and nodded. "I know. But he deserves better."

Malachi stood and took their bowls, putting them in a bucket to be washed. "You've had a hard ride. I've made places for you to sleep—nothing fancy, but hopefully better than the worst pub you ever stayed in," he added with a faint smile. "Get some rest. I'll stay up and research. In the morning, we'll see what can be done."

"Thank you," Ridge said, raising his head. "I know you're taking a risk helping us like this."

"I have my own reasons to want the Witch Lord defeated," Malachi said. "So we have a common enemy. Now rest, and we'll deal with everything else in the morning."

CHAPTER TWELVE

Rett could accept the nightmares. They came with being an assassin. No matter how well-deserved, taking a life scarred the killer. That proved true even when the death was sanctioned by the king. Rett had been a soldier before he became a Shadow. In war, the threat was immediate, dire. An assassin killed in cold blood, a carefully considered murder, usually after having watched the mark long enough to get to know their habits, their routine.

That kind of calculation damaged an assassin, no matter how necessary the mission.

But before, when Rett woke from a nightmare, he knew where the edges of the dream blurred and reality took over. Now, those edges were hard to find, and the boundaries kept shifting. The vile mixtures Doctor had forced on him, pouring the liquids down his throat when all else failed, left Rett feeling loose in his own body as if flesh and bone were a badly tailored suit that no longer fit.

He expected to awaken in a place he vaguely remembered as real—a windowless room, Doctor and Duke, a table spread with instruments of the torturer's craft. At first, when the drugs wore off, he came back to himself, tied to a chair, hungry and hurting. As the questioning went on, those returns happened less often and lasted for a shorter time.

Sounds, touch, and scents became excruciatingly intense, and Rett felt swept away on a wave of sensation. A voice kept asking questions, interrupting the wave. Rett knew he couldn't answer. He didn't remember why, except that someone would be upset—and while he didn't recall a face or a name, he knew gut-deep that he couldn't let that person down.

So he ignored the voice, even when coaxing turned to threats and then to shouts. He pulled back when punches flew, to a safe hiding place in his mind that blunted the discomfort.

Between the waves of sound and colors, when the sweep of impressions waned, his skin itched, his head throbbed like it would burst, and his body thrummed with pain.

Then he felt something cold and wet spread over his skin. His heart stuttered and breath came hard. *I'm dying,* he thought, welcoming the release. Slipping free of his body except for a thin tether, Rett found Edvard and flew to see Lorella. Somewhere along the way, he met Tom, a monk who liked books. For a little while, the pain faded—

Until he slammed back inside himself, worse than before, and prayed to any god that would listen to let him die.

The cycle repeated, but this time Rett knew something had changed. The lines mooring him to his body had shifted, loosened even more. Now his body seemed as unreal as everything else, and he couldn't remember why he had cared about returning to his aching bones and uncomfortable skin.

Except... I thought I came home. For a brief time, Rett heard Ridge's voice and Henri's worried fussing. He had opened his eyes and glimpsed Ridge right in front of him, at a cabin, the last place that had been real. Ridge had looked frantic, begging Rett to stay. But a wave crested, and Rett had to go...

Dark dreams came, and monsters chased him. He thought he remembered rousing enough for someone to pour an odd tea into his mouth. Not poison, though Rett had braced for that. This new mixture made the voices quieter, pushed the dreams back, and helped him find a twilight place between the hallucinations and more pleasant illusions.

Then there were horses, and they were riding long past dark, and Rett heard urgent whispers and Ridge's voice, coaxing him to stay on his horse. He felt sore enough to believe that at least some of those memories were true. They came to a place where something powerful and unseen made him shiver and want to run. Except that a warm lethargy stole over him, and doing anything seemed like too much effort.

I don't hurt as much. Maybe if I stay still, I'll just fade away. He floated, tired and accepting until the darkness of sleep took him. For the first time in a long while, his dreams were peaceful. Painless. Not drenched in blood.

Rett thought he could like it here.

When he woke, Edvard sat on the floor next to him. Rett was in a nest of blankets and didn't recognize his surroundings. Some of the fog that shrouded his mind had cleared, enough that he could access the slight psychic ability that enabled him to hear Edvard in his mind, thanks to the coin hidden deep in his pocket. Poison, pain, and exhaustion had blocked that since his capture. *Are you real?* he asked Edvard.

"I'm a ghost. Real enough."

Where am I?

"Safe. For now."

Rett sat up and realized that his body remained prone. *So, I'm dreaming.*

A door opened, and Rett scrambled away from his sleeping form and into the shadows. Edvard vanished. A man entered, lifting the lantern to have a better look at where Rett lay.

Ridge. Rett stepped out of the shadows. *I'm here. I'm right here. Hey, look at me!*

Ridge knelt next to Rett's form and gently shook his ankle. "Rett. Are you in there? Come on, wake up."

Rett returned to overlay himself with his form and tried to respond. Nothing moved.

"You need to wake up and eat something," Ridge said, voice scratchy and heavy with worry. "You're too skinny. Gotta get you better."

Ridge ran a hand over his face. Rett had thought his friend looked haggard before, but now Ridge looked stretched past his limits.

"This is all my fault," Ridge said. "I should have stayed at Sommerelle and looked harder for you. But they said all the bodies they could recover were accounted for. I'm so sorry. If I'd realized sooner that you were still alive, those assholes wouldn't have had their hands on you for so long. It wouldn't have gotten this bad."

Ridge sucked in a breath. "We brought you to Malachi. If this doesn't work..." He didn't finish the thought, but from his expression, Rett could guess the rest.

I want to come back. I'm trying.

Ridge patted Rett's still form on the knee and then stood, taking the lantern with him. He left the door open a crack, so a faint shaft of light streamed in from outside.

Edvard's ghost gradually took form again next to Rett.

You can see me? Rett asked. Edvard nodded. *Why can't they?*

"*Because we're in your mind,*" Edvard replied.

Maybe Tom could help. His library—Rett stepped away from his sleeping form once more. He moved around the walls of the room, but nothing opened to him. Before, he hadn't even needed to think about going; he just appeared in Tom's library.

"*There's magic keeping you from traveling, I think.*" Edvard watched him with an expression Rett couldn't decipher. "*I heard them say this place is spelled.*"

So, I'm stuck like this? Rett sat back down, feeling like he was sitting on his body instead of inside of it, as he should be. *Am I dying? Is that why my spirit is... loose?*

"*I don't know for sure, but I doubt it's a good thing.*"

If they can't fix me, will I stay like this until my body fails and my spirit fades away? Rett wondered, horrified. He had seen people whose minds were damaged by injury or disease, not dead but barely alive, whose families cared for them until they finally succumbed. *I wouldn't wish that on Ridge and Henri. But what other choice is there? I'd sooner they take a blade to my throat than leave me in the asylum.*

With nowhere to go and no way to make himself heard, Rett tried to settle back into his body, concentrating on moving a finger or toe or just willing his eyes to open, without luck.

The effort exhausted him, and when Rett woke again, he heard a man's voice nearby. *I've heard him before. Malachi?*

Rett was still not able to move his body, but he tried to call out mentally to the necromancer the way he had—unsuccessfully—attempted to contact Ridge.

"I know you're nearby," Malachi said to the empty room as he hung a lantern on a peg and brought in a basket filled with items. "The man who tortured you did more violence to your spirit by ignorance than he could have done with malice. You're fragmented, and I need to spool you back together while we cleanse away the poison. This probably won't be pleasant."

Rett tried to shout and whistle, anything to let Malachi know he heard him, but since the man didn't answer him directly, Rett knew his efforts fell short.

"You survived the immediate effects of the ointment, both when it was given to you and then when the worst of the poison wore off. That's a start," Malachi continued, and Rett figured he had decided to narrate what was going on.

"It's a powerful drug, and it's still in your system, along with several others they dosed you with." A low growl to Malachi's voice suggested his anger at Doctor and Duke. "This is what happens when spiteful children try to pretend they're real witches."

Malachi began his preparations, placing candles, setting a line of salt around the edges of the room, chalking sigils on the floor and walls. "I'm going to start by undoing the spells that were laid on you," Malachi said. "Need to take them one at a time. There's a binding spell, a truth spell, and another spell to break your will. Damn, this is dark shit."

He paused, passing the flat of his palm over Rett's head and chest, skimming a few inches above his body without touching. "The magic is odd. The witch took shortcuts—probably placed the spell through a relic or cursed object. Might mean he didn't want to do it in person."

Malachi leaned forward and tugged at the leather strap around Rett's neck that held the protective charms they had been given. "Well, that explains why it isn't as bad as it could be. These amulets actually worked—as much as they could against what was done to you. It would have been worse without them. If the witch had been present, he would have sensed them. Your captors had no idea what the charms were for."

Malachi's voice was soft. "I'm a necromancer. I know your soul is present. I can sense the damage to your life force. That energy needs to heal and bond again with the rest of you before you can return."

Rett found himself nodding and realized that whatever his current form, Malachi couldn't see his movement.

"If you can hear me ... don't fight what I'm going to do, even if it scares you. Even if it hurts. If you can work with me, it will go better."

Rett wondered where Ridge and Henri were. Probably banished from the room by Malachi, so he could work uninterrupted.

Rett laid back down, settling into the shape on the bed that was—and wasn't—him. He waited, trying to be calm, but although he was disembodied, fear thrummed through him.

Malachi ground something with a mortar and pestle that smelled like the forest. He sprinkled powders of differing colors and scents into the mixture, then dipped his thumb into the concoction and smeared it across Rett's forehead.

Rett steeled himself for the dizzying disorientation the other ointment had caused, relieved when that didn't occur. The smell calmed him, and his skin felt pleasantly warm where the mixture was applied.

Malachi chanted in a language Rett didn't recognize. At first, Rett tried to hang onto every word, hoping to make out the intention. He felt power build like a storm within the small room's stone walls and wondered if he might be struck with lightning. The air crackled with energy, sparking here and there, and Rett watched with a mixture of fear and fascination.

Once Malachi started, he didn't stop except to sip from a glass bottle now and again when his voice went raspy. Sometimes he walked around Rett to the left, and at other times he reversed his course or stood in one place. His arms hung at his sides unless he read from a book, but now and again, he motioned with his hands in strange gestures that seemed like a language of its own.

Rett appreciated the comfort of Malachi's voice, although the man was someone he barely knew. Rett had been alone for too long, and many of the other voices had not been kind. He focused his attention on the strange words, willing them to make a difference.

Sometimes, Rett thought he heard Ridge and Henri, but he couldn't make out what they were saying. *Perhaps they're listening in the hallway.* He felt better knowing they were safe and nearby.

Malachi continued to speak, sometimes chanting, sometimes nearly singing. Rett couldn't be certain, but he thought the mage spoke in various languages, none of them familiar, some more melodic than others. Candle smoke and incense mingled with the tang of exotic powders and strange liquids. Now and again, Malachi leaned over him, fingers working in an intricate, esoteric pattern, and Rett wondered if he imagined the traces of light in the air, green, blue, and gold.

At first, nothing happened. Rett didn't feel any different, and panic rose in his chest. He willed himself to stay still, glad that at the least Malachi's presence staved off the nightmares.

Then gradually Rett felt the numbness in his tongue subside, an unpleasant tingle he hadn't earlier noticed. Next, his chest relaxed as if invisible bands had snapped free. Just as he gulped in a free breath, sudden pain lanced behind his eyes as if a blade thrust through his skull.

Nothing existed except fire and agony, searing along every nerve, blazing through his head, an out-of-control wildfire threatening to take away breath and consciousness. Distantly, he heard screaming and thought it might be him.

Voices sounded again, outside the room.

"What's he doing?"

"You can't go in there. You promised."

"Yeah, well, I'm not going to stand here while he kills him!"

"Go in there, and you'll be the one who ends up killing Rett."

Henri and Ridge again, arguing. Rett noted it in an off-hand way as if it didn't pertain to him, feeling untethered once more like after a few glasses of too-potent absinthe.

The screaming stopped. Rett could feel some of the results of Malachi's magic in his body, but he still felt separate, disassociated.

Malachi kept chanting, and though Rett had lost track of time, he wondered if the magic required the mage to push himself to the extreme. Rett had heard whispers about forbidden power. How strong was Malachi's magic?

Then to his surprise, Rett saw Malachi in his mind, inside his head in the same way he "saw" Edvard.

Malachi didn't stop his invocation, but he put one hand on Rett's shoulder and gave him a compassionate look, warning that whatever was coming would hurt even worse.

The grip on his shoulder grew burning hot, then freezing cold. Rett felt Malachi's strong fingers sink through his flesh and bone until they touched his essence and then ripped it free. Rett stared at the pulsing glow in Malachi's palm, knowing it was the core of who he was.

Malachi's unfamiliar words took on a threatening tone, commanding, focused on the shell of Rett's body. Dark tendrils crept away from Rett's form, like vermin leaving a cooling corpse. Malachi's voice rose in something Rett knew in his bones was a banishing spell. Light flared so bright he had to protect his eyes. It burned the darkness that had pooled around his body to ash and swept it away on a gust of cold wind.

Rett felt fire consume him yet again as Malachi pushed the glowing, swirling mass in his palm against Rett's chest, where it filled his lungs and jolted his heart, slamming his loosened spirit back into his flesh with a violent collision.

He sat upright in his bed with a sharp intake of breath, overwhelmed with the sensation of being fully back in his body, cleansed of the limitations of spells and the pollution of elixirs.

Malachi hadn't finished. He held a hand over Rett's head, speaking low and gentle, a benediction. Rett felt a shimmer of power thrum through him from head to foot, and in his mind, it glowed golden like the sun.

Rett's heart pounded, and he heaved for breath, but for the first time in weeks, he felt solid, anchored body to spirit, no longer watching himself like an observer.

Malachi murmured the last few words, and then his hand dropped, and his head slumped.

Ridge tore free of Henri's grip in the doorway and sidestepped around Malachi, stopping a pace from Rett's bedside, eyes wide, face pale.

"Are you back?"

Rett managed a tremulous smile. "I think so."

All the tension and worry seemed to drain from Ridge, who looked like he might collapse without the nervous energy of desperation to sustain him. "Good." He pulled Rett into a tight hug as if to assure himself this was real, and Rett was solid.

Rett needed that reassurance just as much.

"Welcome home," Henri said, in a voice strained with emotion.

Rett looked at Malachi with concern. "Are you alright?" he asked, then coughed and realized his throat was sore from screaming.

"I will be. How do you feel?"

"More like myself," Rett said. Now that the worst had been averted, he mostly felt grateful and exhausted.

Kane bustled in, making the small room feel even more crowded. "Malachi and Rett need to eat and rest." He looked to Henri and Ridge. "Go fix food and drink. I'll help Malachi undo the ritual items." Kane gave Rett a look that raked him up and down. "Glad you're back with us," he added with his usual smirking tone.

Ridge spared him one more worried glance as if assuring himself that Rett really was awake and talking, then followed Henri out of the room.

Malachi took a step and staggered. Kane grabbed him by the arm and pulled him over to the wall, not letting go until the mage sank down to sit on the floor.

"I already released the energies," Malachi said, sounding exhausted. "There's nothing special about the items now."

"That's good because growing another head would make it difficult to blend in as a spy," Kane muttered. He snuffed out the candles, rubbed gaps into the chalked sigils, and then carefully picked up the bowl, carrying all of the elements out of the room before he returned for Malachi.

"You need to rest," Kane said, helping Malachi to his feet.

"I'll be fine. I've been worse."

"Let's get you to your room. I'll bring you food." Kane's tone didn't allow for refusal, and to Rett's surprise, Malachi didn't try.

"Thank you." Rett looked up as Malachi headed for the door. "I didn't think I'd make it out alive."

Malachi managed a tired smile. "You're welcome. Your stubbornness played as much of a role as my magic. I almost lost you a couple of times, but you didn't let go."

"I needed to come back."

"It served you well."

Kane didn't assist Malachi but stayed close enough that if the mage faltered, he could step in before the other man slammed to the ground.

Once they were gone, Rett realized he could still see Edvard's faint image in the corner. *I can still see you.*

Edvard nodded. *"You are stronger now than before."*

Funny, because I feel like I'd blow over in a stiff wind.

"I mean your ability. Your Sight."

Who knows what all that stuff did to me? He stifled a yawn, feeling like he could sleep for a week. *I'll figure it out... after I get a little bit of sleep.*

Before he could drift off, Ridge returned with tea and buttered bread. "It's just tea," Ridge assured him when Rett looked askance at the drink. "But whatever concoction Henri brewed up back at the cabin kept you from having fits while we were riding, so he saved our asses again."

Ridge watched in silence as Rett ate, and Rett could almost feel Ridge's fraying self-restraint as he held off asking questions.

"I'm glad you're back," Ridge said, taking the empty cup and plate. "This time, you scared the shit out of me."

"I scared me too," Rett replied with a wan smile. "Where are we?"

Ridge snorted. "Would you believe, Runed Keep?"

Rett raised an eyebrow. "I guess I missed some details along the way."

"Nothing that won't wait until morning. Get some sleep, and then I promise to fill you in. It's just good to have you looking like yourself again."

Rett slid down and settled into bed. "I don't remember much, but thank you for whatever you did to bring me here."

"Can't cause mayhem and save the kingdom without my partner," Ridge answered, standing. "Now—rest. Yell if you need something." He didn't close the door completely, leaving a sliver of light and the distant, muted sound of voices to lull Rett into a deep and remarkably dreamless sleep.

CHAPTER THIRTEEN

"**A**re you sure your head is in the mission?" Kane asked, a no-nonsense look in his eyes. "Because there's been a lot going on lately. There's no shame if you want to put this off a day or two."

"No. We know where Letwick is tonight. Tomorrow he could be gone, and there's no guarantee we'd find him again. We need to finish this," Ridge replied.

Ridge knew that Kane was right to be concerned. Malachi had spent candlemarks stripping away the invisible bonds of magic and poison that remained after they had freed Rett from his captors. They had all been stretched thin, waiting for the outcome. Kane was clearly just as worried about Malachi as Henri and Ridge were about Rett. None of them came through unscathed.

The next morning, when they all finally crawled out of bed, they got answers from Malachi and Rett—about the magics used, the types of potions, and what it meant for Rett's abilities. Ridge worried about the pieces Malachi couldn't explain—how Rett had been able to travel without his body all the way to Harrowmont, why Malachi's necromancy resonated with Rett's very-alive spirit, and the identity of Tom, the mysterious monk.

That last issue gave Ridge pause. Was Tom just a figment of Rett's imagination, creating a safe harbor for himself when the drugs and torture became too much to bear? Or did he exist somewhere, and if so, was he important? Rett swore he had never met the man, and Malachi offered nothing but theories.

Ridge didn't like loose ends or unanswered questions. They caused problems, and their group already had enough trouble to last for a long time. He resolved to give Rett time to recuperate and then go looking for answers.

They were surprised when Gil sent a ghost messenger to Malachi, providing them with Letwick's location. The duke had taken refuge in the hunting lodge of one of the nobles who died the year before, whose family was still quibbling about the inheritance. Since it wasn't hunting season, Ridge guessed Letwick figured the cabin would be empty and far enough from everything to be undisturbed.

Ridge and Kane headed out the next morning, leaving Rett to recuperate with Henri and Malachi.

Ghosts make the best spies. We need to figure out how to keep them working with us.

"The ghosts thought he was here alone," Ridge murmured. "I'd like to confirm that before we go thundering through the doors—in case he has his witch with him."

They silently circled the lodge in opposite directions, meeting up in the large barn that housed only one horse. "Looks like he's by himself," Kane said.

"If he ran the night we rescued Rett and came here, he might have had second thoughts about dragging any of his guards into this," Ridge replied. "After all, it's one thing to do their master's bidding when it was just roughing up a personal enemy. But the duke has to be afraid Rett will implicate him in killing the king. That's a line his guards might not be willing to cross, given the consequences."

"And if the witch is smart, he's long gone, maybe even out of the kingdom by now," Kane said. "I doubt he's all that loyal once money's not involved."

The lodge was a less glamorous and smaller manor house, rustic but still far more comfortable than the homes of regular folk. Though it might be used only a few times a year, it was larger than a normal home or cabin, designed for hunting parties accompanied by servants.

It didn't look like anyone had been here in a long time, and Ridge wondered whether the late owner's death had kept it from being in use the previous season. Clearly, Letwick knew about the lodge, had probably been a guest at some point, and guessed it was unlikely to be inhabited.

I need to find out how Letwick is connected to the previous owner of the lodge. That might turn up some interesting relationships and lead back to the Witch Lord.

"The ghost's information looks right," Kane said, assessing the lodge from the shadows of the barn. "Two doors, stone walls, plenty of windows. Solid, but not a fortress."

"The ghost said Letwick was armed," Ridge replied. "A matchlock and hunting bows."

"He's alone, so he can't shoot at both of us at the same time. One of us runs interference, and the other sneaks in while he's distracted."

"Same as at the castle?" Ridge asked. "I go up and in; you go through the front?"

"If the plan works, why change it?" Kane shrugged.

Ridge stared at the hunting lodge, assessing. "You know, you're right about it not being a fortress. It was built for the people doing the hunting, not being hunted. Do you see how wide the corners are? The windows on either side aren't going to have a full view of the approach. There's no vantage point where someone inside can see all the surrounding ground."

Kane nodded. "Get to the corner, and it's like trying to look at the tip of your nose."

"I'll go up the back corner," Ridge said, pulling out his rope and a new grappling hook from his pack.

"I'll make a fuss coming in from the front. He can't watch us both," Kane added with a grin.

"Just remember how far a matchlock and a hunting bow can fire. I have no desire for Malachi to turn me into a toad for getting you punctured."

"He wouldn't turn you into a toad," Kane replied, taking the warning in stride. "He'd rip out your soul, cast it into the Void, and send you screaming into the Abyss for eternity. Toads are for beginners."

Ridge figured it was probably best not to think too hard about that. Then again, it never hurt to remember that powerful friends could become relentless enemies. Usually, all Ridge had to worry about was being bested in a knife fight. Consorting with mages brought a whole new level of possibilities—and dangers. He resolved to do everything he could to stay on Malachi's good side.

Ridge waited until Kane was in position before he moved, and he was already halfway to the lodge when the first blast of a matchlock broke the forest's silence.

Takes a while to reload unless he's got multiple guns. He can switch to a bow, but if he's firing arrows, there's no one to reload the matchlock.

Ridge reached the corner and threw his hook. This was the second job he'd worked with Kane, counting Rett's rescue. While Kane was good, Ridge missed the near-telepathic familiarity he had with Rett, born from long experience. Kane's reactions were still an unknown, where Ridge and Rett had a lifetime of shared experience to draw from, both as Shadows and before, in the army and orphanage.

Duke Letwick almost killed Rett. He's going to pay. Bringing the king's killer to justice is a bonus.

The climb went fast and easy, and Ridge had no trouble shimmying through a window that opened with disturbing ease. He crouched in the dim interior of the room, listening. The muffled bang of another matchlock shot told him that Letwick's attention was focused elsewhere.

Ridge took a moment to get his bearings, something he'd learned early could make a life or death difference. Letwick was somewhere with a view of the lodge's front. Ridge listened for other footsteps, any evidence that Letwick was not alone despite what the ghost spy said.

When he didn't hear anything except Letwick's loud cursing and the sporadic report of his gun, Ridge drew his knives. *Time to go to work.*

The boxy lodge had a more straightforward layout than palaces or castles. While comfortable and well-equipped, it had been built to be functional without needing to host grand receptions or the offices of functionaries. That meant the third floor would probably be servants' quarters, the second floor was for guest bedrooms, and the first floor almost certainly had gathering spaces for meals and socializing.

Ridge had come in on the third floor, which he had guessed to be the least likely for Letwick to occupy. As a guest, the duke would have had no reason or desire to explore the servants' areas on a prior visit, and they wouldn't offer his accustomed luxury. The first floor didn't provide the same vantage point for defense as the view from the second floor might, so Ridge figured Letwick was probably one floor below him.

He descended the stairs silently, careful to stay at the edges of the steps to avoid squeaky boards. From the dust on the floor and furnishings, he suspected that the lodge had sat unused for even longer than they had guessed.

The stairway from the third floor to the second was not meant for guests to navigate. It was dark and cramped, purely functional. On the bright side, Ridge felt sure that Letwick probably had never paid it any attention, taking for granted that whenever he summoned a servant they would appear, as if by magic.

Now that worked to Ridge's advantage. The stairway door opened into an empty utility room with a second stairway descending to the first floor. Another shot rang out, and it sounded like it came from nearby, confirming his guess about where Letwick had taken a sniper position.

Letwick's continuing shots meant Kane had managed to elude him thus far. Ridge eased the door open and slipped into the hallway. The back portion of the corridor looked untouched, while the front part closer to the grand main staircase showed obvious signs of occupation. Footprints disturbed the thick dust, and outside one room sat empty bottles and jugs, proof that Letwick had made camp.

Ridge waited until the matchlock boomed again, then while his ears still rang and he figured Letwick was even more deafened, he ran for the door, kicked it open, dove, and rolled.

The room smelled of gunpowder and candle smoke. An arrow thudded into the wall where Ridge had been just seconds before, and Ridge never stopped moving, knowing how quickly a skilled archer could fire. He had no idea how good Letwick was with a bow, but he didn't want to find out the hard way.

Letwick fired again, and the arrow sank deep into the table Ridge knocked over for cover. Ridge popped up long enough to throw a knife while Letwick's focus was on drawing his bow. The knife blade lodged in the duke's right shoulder. Letwick dropped the bow, cursing like a sailor, and reached for a sword that lay on a nearby table. It seemed he intended to go down fighting.

Ridge had no intention of killing Letwick until the man confessed his role in Kristoph's murder and named his co-conspirators. Before Letwick could skewer Ridge's hiding place with his blade, Ridge hurled another throwing knife that cut into the man's right thigh just above the knee. Letwick dropped to the floor, bleeding freely.

Ridge heard the front door slam open, and then someone— hopefully Kane—was taking the stairs several steps at a time. Ridge braced for trouble, knives at the ready, but then Kane appeared in the doorway, looking like he'd had a fine game of chase.

"I see you found him," Kane said.

Letwick growled and tried to get to his feet, but his knee wouldn't hold him, and as he fell, Kane kicked the sword out of his hand while Ridge removed the bow, arrows, and matchlock from reach.

"Do you know who I am? I'll have you hanged for attacking me!" Weston, Duke of Letwick, kept his pride and bluster, even blood-soaked and on his knees.

"You're not leaving this room," Ridge said, drawing another knife as he moved closer. Kane retrieved the duke's weapons, and reloaded the matchlock, then stood back and kept the gun trained on Letwick. At this distance, he couldn't miss.

"What do you want? Money? I'll pay you. Favors? I can arrange whatever you want." Having failed to intimidate, Letwick fell back on negotiation.

"What I want? King Kristoph, alive. And my partner, un-tortured. Make both of those happen, and we'll go away. Might even find you a healer." Ridge's eyes narrowed. "How about it? Do we have a deal?"

Letwick's expression darkened. "Kristoph was the last in a long line of thieves. His family stole the crown from my ancestor. I just wanted what's rightfully ours!"

"Who else was involved?" Ridge brought the tip of the knife up beneath Letwick's chin, touching the point gently to his throat. "Who else among the nobles was involved in the plot to kill Kristoph?"

Letwick smirked. "Kristoph had more enemies than you know. You can kill me, but it won't change what happened. It won't stop what's to come. Maybe I won't be the Letwick crowned king, but my family will regain the throne, and there's nothing you can do to stop it."

He looked so triumphant in his defiance that Ridge wondered if the man didn't realize his peril.

"We know that the Witch Lord—the man who calls himself Yefim Makary—is a Letwick. He's nobody special, no one touched by the gods. Just a liar and a swindler," Ridge baited.

Despite his situation, Letwick jerked like he wanted to throw himself at Ridge, held back by his injuries.

"Where's your witch?"

Letwick made a rude noise. "That ungrateful wretch! He's probably across the border by now. I'll kill him if you don't."

Ridge drew a thin line with the blade over Letwick's jugular, enough to let the man know that he meant what he threatened.

"I want to know who else among the nobles was involved. You've already lost everything—we'll make sure your lands and title are forfeit. Don't you want your collaborators to get the punishment they deserve? Or are you the fool they left holding the bag?"

Letwick's face reddened with apoplexy, and his eyes looked like they might bug out of his face. "You have no right—"

Ridge looked to Kane. "What do you think? If you shoot him in the belly, it'll take him a while to die. Nasty way to go. But he'll have plenty of time to talk before he begs us to slit his throat to stop the pain. Do you think that might make him share some names?"

The spark in Kane's eyes said he was on to Ridge's tactic. "You know, I watched a man take three days to die with his guts on the outside of his skin. Then his shit got into his blood, and fever burned him up from the inside. He twisted like a man on the gallows the whole time, out of his mind with pain."

Ridge had purposely looked away from Letwick as they spoke, but a glance out of the corner of his eye registered the duke's horror, as the man finally seemed to realize how grave his situation had become.

"Wait! I can give you names."

Ridge turned and raised an eyebrow. "Start talking. If we think you're holding out the important pieces, he'll shoot you."

The duke babbled, and Ridge made mental note of the names mentioned. If Letwick was to be believed, a worrisome number of the lesser nobility were implicated in supporting the Witch Lord's insurrection.

"Who will Makary put forward for the crown once you're dead?" Ridge asked.

Letwick paled. "My brother Alston. He would be next after me if the line of succession got that far."

Which brought them back to the muddy issue of who the legitimate heir would be since Kristoph died without a child. Ridge guessed that royal genealogists were arguing the matter and would continue until a suitable candidate with the right lineage was selected. He strongly doubted the Witch Lord's followers intended to be that patient.

"They shortened the line, you know." Letwick panted with pain as he shifted on his bleeding leg, then groaned when the movement jarred the knife in his shoulder.

"What do you mean?" Ridge's sharp tone sprang from the sinking feeling in his gut that there was another treachery they hadn't yet uncovered.

"The line of succession," Letwick said, nervously licking his lips. Ridge could see in the man's eyes that he no longer had any illusions about making it out alive. Perhaps he hoped that confessing his secrets would lead to some sort of absolution, or at least a quicker death.

"Makary has been working on it, quietly, behind the scenes. Accidents happening to people in Kristoph's line. Fatal illnesses. Nothing too unusual, not too close together. The deaths looked natural, but they weren't. There are hardly any true candidates from Kristoph's bloodline left," Letwick went on. "Any that remain are so far removed, I don't think the Council would consider them." A taut smile touched his lips. "So perhaps we've won, after all."

Ridge exchanged a look with Kane. "I'd love for him to testify to the Council of Nobles. Might get Rett and me off the hook for Kristoph's murder."

Kane shook his head. "With Kristoph dead and Burke missing, Makary's followers are likely to have control of the Council. Even if you made it to the palace without getting arrested, they'd never let you present the evidence. You'd be executed, and Letwick will still end up with his throat slit."

Much as Ridge wished he could argue, he knew Kane was right. He withdrew the writ from his jacket, the last one signed by King Kristoph, verbally filling in Letwick's name, authorizing summary execution. "Weston Letwick, you are charged with regicide, treason, sedition, kidnapping, and the torture and near-murder of one of the King's Shadows. By the power of this writ, in the name of the king, I pronounce your life to be forfeit."

"You can go—" Letwick snarled.

The rest of his curse fell silent as the blade slashed deep across his throat, cutting through to the spine. Letwick's body pulsed blood, remained upright for a few seconds, then toppled and lay with the head tipped at an impossible angle. Ridge took one of Letwick's arrows and stabbed it through the writ into the plaster wall so that it hung above the body for all to see.

"Well, they're not going to wonder who killed him," Kane observed.

"They weren't going to wonder, no matter how I did it," Ridge replied, looking down at the dead man. "This doesn't change anything. Kristoph is dead, Rett nearly died, and we're still outlaws. Makary is out there somewhere, alive and scheming with supporters. We haven't found Letwick's witch. The succession is in chaos. It's not over yet—but at least Kristoph and Rett are avenged."

"Does it make you feel any better?" For once, Kane's voice held none of its usual sarcasm. Ridge figured the spy had faced the desire for revenge a time or two himself.

"No. Not really," Ridge replied, utterly candid. He met Kane's gaze and felt sure the other man understood from bitter experience. "Doesn't fix a damn thing, but it's not as bad as leaving things undone."

Ridge bent to reclaim his knives, then took the matchlock, bow, and arrows. Good weapons were hard to find.

Kane turned to leave. "Come on," he said. "They'll be waiting for us at the tower. We have plans to make."

CHAPTER FOURTEEN

"You did it." Rett looked from Ridge to Kane and couldn't begin to name all of the emotions tangled in his chest at their recount of the fight with Letwick. "You avenged Kristoph."

"And we kicked the ass of the guy behind your kidnapping," Ridge added, with an expression suggesting that was the most important aspect.

"I'm surprised Letwick got personally involved like that," Malachi said, leaning away from the table where little remained of the venison stew and fresh bread they had consumed for dinner. "He could have just sat back and let Makary deliver the crown to him."

"He might have been impatient, or so sure of victory that he got careless," Henri suggested.

"Or Makary could have goaded him into it, expecting him to fail, if he preferred a different candidate," Kane speculated.

"Maybe," Ridge said. "I guess that's the next step—sorting out the snakes."

"You might be interested to know that I can't summon Kristoph's ghost," Malachi said.

"Is that unusual?" Rett asked.

Malachi nodded. "Kristoph and I didn't part on the best terms, but such disagreements tend to fade when a spirit crosses the Veil. Death changes a person's perspective," he added with a wry expression. "He cared about what was best for the kingdom, and at the end, he had to know that someone murdered him. Gil and Lorella are fine mediums, but I'm more powerful, making me Kristoph's best bet to tell us anything of importance."

"Like who should succeed him?" Ridge's head came up sharply.

"That, and other secrets that might be helpful," Malachi said. "But Kristoph's spirit is bound. I can't reach him."

"Bound?" Rett echoed. "Who can do that? You just said you were the most powerful necromancer in the kingdom."

"I don't know." Malachi's tone sent a chill down Rett's spine.

"The only reason to bind a ghost would be to keep it from telling secrets," Kane said. "I've heard of spell work to do that, but not that would hold against a mage like Malachi."

"So either we've underestimated Makary's magic, or he has a high-powered mage in his corner," Ridge replied. "Maybe more than one."

"I can't come up with any other explanation," Malachi said. "But I don't like the implications."

"What now?" Rett asked. He and Ridge hadn't had a lot of time to talk after Ridge returned from hunting down Letwick. But after they had assured each other that they were, in fact, alive, little discussion had been needed to agree that they hadn't finished their real mission of stopping the Witch Lord.

Malachi's gaze went from Ridge to Rett. "You have no official position. You're outlaws. But you still plan to go after Makary and the Witch Lord's supporters?"

Rett and Ridge exchanged a glance, then nodded in silent agreement.

"If we don't, who will?" Ridge asked. "Kristoph had his faults, but he was a decent king. Anyone Makary puts on the throne won't be. Now that we know Makary has his hooks into so many of the nobles, that means no one is going to continue investigating Kristoph's death. They're going to write it off as solved—blaming us—and that will be the end of it. Unless we keep digging."

"There are good people in this kingdom who deserve better than Makary's puppet on the throne. The honest guards and the decent Shadows and the nobles who aren't assholes—they deserve better too," Rett said. "I don't care if anyone ever knows who helped stop Makary, as long as he gets stopped."

"Where else would we go?" Henri shrugged as if the question concerned which pub to choose for dinner. "We have a price on our heads in Landria, and I don't doubt word would spread to the neighboring kingdoms. Retiring to the countryside isn't going to work for us until this is settled. And if I'm going to die, I'd rather do it with my boots on and my eyes open."

"Have I mentioned that you have an exceptionally bloodthirsty valet?" Kane asked with a chuckle. Henri's cheeks colored, but his smile suggested he was flattered.

"Wouldn't have it any other way," Ridge replied.

Malachi placed a large, shallow bowl in the center of the table after they cleared away their plates from dinner. He poured water into the container and let it settle into stillness. As Rett watched in fascination, the mage's fingers twitched in a complex pattern over the water, and he spoke a few words of power.

When the others looked into the bowl, they saw Gil and Luc. Malachi looked up. "Gil wanted to make sure you got here safely, and I thought they should be part of the conversation since they have a stake in the game. It wasn't wise for them to be here in the flesh."

"Glad you made it," Gil said, his voice clear even if it sounded distant. Their images were visible on the surface of the liquid. Luc stood behind him, his military background evident in his stance, wearing a simple black outfit of tunic and trews. Gil looked the part of a man of leisure, clad in an expensive-looking waistcoat. "I'll be relaying the outcome of our conversation to Lady Sally Anne when we come to a decision."

Ridge and Rett turned to look at Malachi and Kane. "Decision?" Rett echoed.

The look that passed between Malachi and Kane reminded Rett that he and Ridge weren't the only ones who could have an entire conversation without speaking aloud.

"One of the reasons I've been helping you is because, as you've pointed out, while Kristoph wasn't perfect, other kings have been much worse."

"He imprisoned you here," Ridge said quietly. "You've made it work, but he didn't mean for you to be comfortable."

An expression passed over Malachi's face that Rett couldn't interpret. "Kristoph sought to lock away his grief over the death of his wife and stillborn son when he sent me to the tower. Such things never work out as intended. I let him believe it because it served my purposes. And, as you've noted, I have made it work." His glance at Kane spoke volumes.

"But we have no desire to test what Makary would do with the power of a throne," Kane added. "I will not spy for him, and he would seek to control Malachi and force his service."

"We feel the same," Gil said, and Luc nodded, both of them looking grim but resolved.

"And Lady Sally Anne?" Rett asked.

"She says that you already know what use Makary wanted to make of the children's abilities," Luc said. "As well as others in her protection. She has no love for Makary."

"Then I guess we've got our own little revolution brewing." A smile spread across Ridge's face.

"We can't move openly," Kane said. "We don't have any official power. And we may not have any allies beyond the ones we've named. You do realize there is little chance of succeeding."

Rett grinned. "Welcome to the Shadows. That's what we do."

ABOUT THE AUTHOR

Gail Z. Martin writes urban fantasy, epic fantasy, and steampunk for Solaris Books, Orbit Books, Falstaff Books, SOL Publishing, and Darkwind Press. Urban fantasy series include *Deadly Curiosities* and the *Night Vigil* (Sons of Darkness). Epic fantasy series include *Darkhurst, The Chronicles of The Necromancer, The Fallen Kings Cycle, The Ascendant Kingdoms Saga, and The Assassins of Landria.* Under her urban fantasy MM paranormal romance pen name of Morgan Brice, she has five series (*Witchbane, Badlands, Kings of the Mountain, Fox Hollow,* and *Treasure Trail*) with more books and series to come.

Co-authored with Larry N. Martin are *Iron and Blood*, the first novel in the Jake Desmet Adventures series and the *Storm and Fury* collection; and the *Spells, Salt, & Steel*: New Templars series (Mark Wojcik, monster hunter), as well as *Wasteland Marshals* and *Cauldron: The Joe Mack Adventures.*

Gail's work has appeared in more than forty US/UK anthologies. Newest anthologies include: *The Weird Wild West, Gaslight and Grimm, Baker Street Irregulars, Hath no Fury, Legends, Across the Universe, Release the Virgins, Tales from the Old Black Ambulance, Witches Warriors and Wise Women, Afterpunk: Steampunk Tales of the Afterlife. Christmas at Caynham Castle,* and *Trick or Treat at Caynham Castle.*

Join the Shadow Alliance street team so you never miss a new release! Get all the scoop first + giveaways + fun stuff! Also where Gail and Larry get their beta readers and Launch Team! https://www.facebook.com/groups/435812789942761

Find out more at www.GailZMartin.com, on Twitter @ GailZMartin, at her blog at www.DisquietingVisions.com, on

Goodreads https://www.goodreads.com/GailZMartin and on Bookbub https://www.bookbub.com/profile/gail-z-martin.

Join the newsletter and get free excerpts at http://eepurl.com/dd5XLj On Instagram: https://www.instagram.com/morganbrice-author/ on Pinterest: http://www.pinterest.com/gzmartin

Gail is also a con-runner for ConTinual, the online, ongoing multi-genre convention that never ends. www.Facebook.com/Groups/ConTinual

ABOUT THE PUBLISHER

This book is published on behalf of the author by the Ethan Ellenberg Literary Agency.
https://ethanellenberg.com
Email: agent@ethanellenberg.com

Printed in Great Britain
by Amazon

56917476R00123